Briar Patch

Mike D. Jones

authorHOUSE®

AuthorHouse™
1663 Liberty Drive
Bloomington, IN 47403
www.authorhouse.com
Phone: 1-800-839-8640

This book is a work of fiction. People, places, events, and situations are the product of the author's imagination. Any resemblance to actual persons, living or dead, or historical events, is purely coincidental.

First published by AuthorHouse 6/17/2010

ISBN: 978-1-4520-0696-3 (e)
ISBN: 978-1-4520-0695-6 (sc)

Library of Congress Control Number: 2010904737

Printed in the United States of America
Bloomington, Indiana

This book is printed on acid-free paper.

Registered with the Writer's Guild West #1351593
For additional titles, please visit www.redriverpublications.com

Introduction

Down through the ages all cultures have had their historians, chroniclers, wisemen, etc. American Indians often had certain tribal members who were considered wise. Their counsel and advice did not go unheeded. They were known as Sachems. Poets speak of the wise ones as sages and bible scholars study about prophets. Other groups of wise are known as oracles and Shakespeare called the mentally gifted by the name of soothsayer.

Almost every locale has some sort of observer known for their wisdom. The wise one from our town was Mr. Ladoit Shagnasty. There is an old adage that says, "You don't know if someone is a real prophet until their predictions come true." Until those moments of truth arise they are merely loudmouths, eccentrics or busy bodies. The eccentric that practiced his observational predictions in our small town has matured to full flower as a prophet and sage as time has proven.

Four early observations that come to mind are:

1.) Living in this town doesn't give you much to see, but what you hear sure makes up for it.

2.) There is an overly abundant supply of oddballs around here for such a small place.

The third observation went from the general to the specific. It was not overly delicate or tactful.

3.) In among these oddballs there also seems to be an assortment of nut cases, perverts and village idiots.

4.) A town of twenty times more population could not match the assortment of personalities in this place.

Times and tide has proven these observations accurate. It should also be noted that Briar Patch also had its share of "dear hearts and gentle folk." They just didn't get noticed much. Peyton Place was not known for its learned ones and leading citizens and neither was Briar Patch.

Teachers, clergy, and the police can vouch for that observation. Ladoit Shagnasty noted that most of the antics of the Briar Patch characters would not be believable to the naïve and those with tender ears.

With this being said, here then is his story..............

FIREWATER BARSTOOL

Firewater Barstool

Firewater was the only barber in town. His only formal schooling for cutting hair consisted of sweeping out the shop for a <u>real</u> barber. He was "let go" from this position due to his habit of drinking all the shop's hair tonic with an alcoholic content. It was rumored that he could only cut hair good when he was intoxicated. He began to hallucinate and see things that other people could not (but his breath smelled good). After an early retirement he deteriorated even more. No one liked his haircuts, but he was the only game in town. Firewater had, in the past, drug people off the sidewalk to help him catch the "little green men" he saw pouring out of a clock on the mantle. He would run around the shop, knocking down all sorts of bottles, attempting to capture these little green men who he insisted were "Taking the place" (maybe they were from Mexico).

After Firewater retired, he lived with his mother in a neighboring town. On the day in question, a school bus full of grade school children had stopped near his house to load some students. The night before this incident, Barstool had come home drunk and fallen in the drainage ditch. The ditch was muddy and he was too incapacitated to climb out. Having wallowed in the mud all night, he presented quiet a sight to youngsters unaccustomed to such exposure. All eyes on the bus looked like a stump full of young owls. He and his mother were shouting back and fourth from her front porch to the ditch. She would pray loudly, "Oh Lord please forgive my poor drunk son." He would answer back, "Don't tell him I'm drunk, tell him I'm sick."

BANDIT HANGING

Bandit Hanging

"Bandit" was not the man's real name. He earned this title by being the only mechanic in town. Like Firewater Barstool, he had a captive income. He charged outrageous prices for his service. His arrogance included ignoring his customers for the first thirty minutes after they entered his garage. Although his customers despised him, they never called him "Bandit" to his face! However, if anyone passing through town needed a mechanic, they were referred to "Mr. Bandit Hanging", where they would always make the fatal mistake of addressing him this way. Bandit enjoyed exploiting the village idiots in town for his amusement. There was a never-ending supply of these candidates. Like Firewater Barstool, Bandit was also an alcoholic. The major difference being that Bandit drank <u>after</u> work. He had a pinched, angular face whose smile never reached his eyes.

RUFF   BRIER

Ruff Brier

Ruff was a crazy woman of undetermined age. She wore rags until they literally rotted off of her. To keep her shoes together she wrapped them in sacks, secured with heavy twine. The woman's hair had never seen a brush or comb and a bath was unknown. When she spoke, she shouted and cussed like a sailor with every breath. Locals encouraged this outrageous behavior for the novel entertainment. Ruff lived in a shack two blocks from what passed for downtown. The shack was crammed full of old newspapers to the ceiling and secured with clothesline wires to keep it in place. Actual living space was a trail leading to what used to be the kitchen, with enough room to turn around. Then a branch trail to reach the bed. The property still boasted a "shit house" during the days of indoor plumbing. Ruff spent most of her home hours sitting on the front porch so she could cuss at the passing traffic and wave a butcher knife at anyone who shouted back at her. She frequently went to town and entered stores and shops demanding food, etc. and cussing at the top of her lungs. The town took care of her needs because no one else would. She came to see this as her God given right and her belligerence and unreasonable behavior knew no bounds. Ruff also enjoyed revealing her extensive sexual history to anyone who would care to listen. A typical conversation with Ruff went something like this:

Upon entering a local grocery store, Ruff would shout; "God damn it! I'm hungry, give me something to eat right now"! One day the preacher stopped by her shack and ask, "Ruff, what happened to that picture of Jesus I gave you?" Her response was, "Oh, the god-damn rats et a hole in the son-of-a-bitch and I had to throw it away." Ruff's late husband, another nut, got in a fight with someone of equal IQ using a couple of hoes. The hoe fight took place over a barbwire fence near her property. Ruff's husband was killed outright at the scene. She would tell the story and add, "That son-of-a-bitch is in hell right now!" Additional incidents are all too numerous to list here.

AXEL FENDER

Axel Fender

Mr. Axel Fender was one of the lucky people who had enough mechanical ability to not need Bandit Hanging's services. He built his own hotrod and was also an Elvis impersonator. No talent, just tried to look the part. Axel was above average in strength, so he was not bothered by the predators. Good athletic ability was wasted as it was combined with a very non- aggressive personality. He did however, possess great quickness and deadly combat training. Although slow to anger, he could be nasty if provoked.

Axel pretended not to see people in public so he would not have to wave or say hi. He wasn't aloof, just very shy. This strange behavior even extended to his best friends (a sort of "glitch or tic" in his personality). Axel only lived a block from Ruff's shack. He enjoyed baiting her for the screaming and cussing he received. Driving by and lobbing a cherry bomb (the largest firecracker available) at her house was great sport. She would always run out swinging the butcher knife cussing a blue streak. On this particular day, he was driving toward her place and trying to light the bomb at the same time. He became so involved in getting it lit and laughing at how funny this would be that he ran off the road and the bomb went off in his car.

No one in town would let their daughters go out with Axel because of his long family history of prison. Although Axel himself never got in trouble, he was unfairly labeled by an accident of birth. It was probably this fact which caused Axel to breed out of his species. Cattle usually being the subject of choice. No one minded much because Axel was very discreet. He did not brag about his conquests and usually operated at night. Besides, there were much worse things in town to worry about than a nocturnal cowpoke...... things like Mr. Catshit Looney.

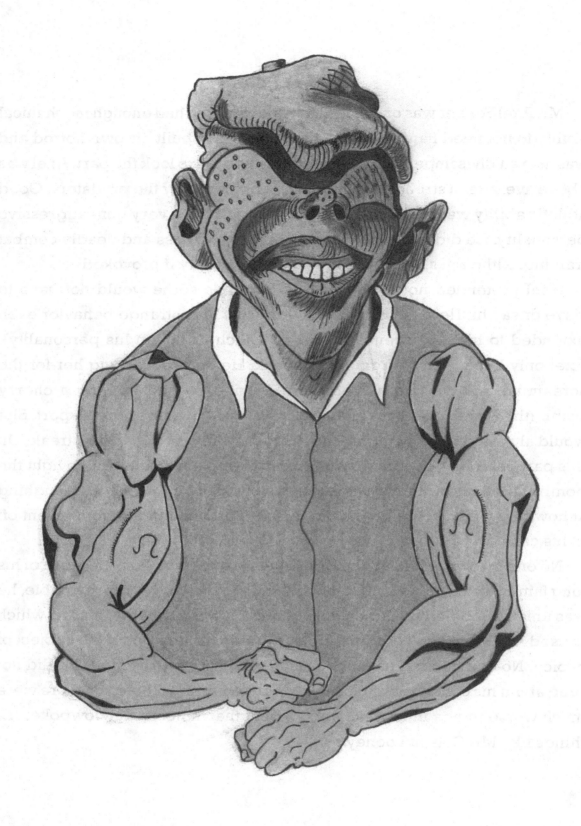

CATSHIT LOONEY

Catshit Looney

In a town blessed with an over abundance of "village idiots" he was a stand out! A retarded sadist with freaky strength and enough speed to catch and hurt anyone smaller than himself. Catshit was basically an extortionist. If he needed money he would mow someone's yard. It did not matter if they had not asked him to mow it, or, if in fact it ever needed mowing at all. One would see him in their yard and pray they had enough money to buy him off. Elderly people on fixed incomes were especially at risk, as they could not stand up to him physically and could sometimes not pay him. The only recourse under these conditions was to lock the doors, hide, and hope he would go away. As Catshit matured and became even stronger and faster, he graduated to not only inflicting pain on anyone he could catch, to developing a sexual interest in his victims. Age and gender was no barrier. In a town with no law this soon became a serious problem. Much of the blame for this can be laid at the door of Bandit Hanging. Bandit supplied Catshit with "porno" material and he was occasionally seen masturbating in incomplete hiding by local citizens. People said, "We should feel sorry for Catshit", but it's hard to remember that when he's twisting your arm out of place or worse! Catshit was eventually permanently incarcerated for "cornholing" (anal assaulting) one of the locals.

B.O. SHARP

B. O. Sharp

Mr. B. O. Sharp came from a very large family. So large in fact that the parents ceased to name the children, they just gave them initials. No one else in the family was anything like him. B. O. was a genetic throwback to some remote Neanderthal relative. No one who saw him ever came away unimpressed! Not a tall man, he was about average height. His bodyweight was around three hundred pounds. Shoulder width was close to three feet and upper body thickness was approximately two feet at chest level. The possessor of colossal natural strength, only two other men in town could stay close to him and one of them was a giant. Unfortunately this ability was coupled to a low IQ. Third grade was as far as B. O. achieved before it was realized that he was only suited for farm labor. Lifting tractors and pulling engine blocks out of cars with just his hands was not a problem for him. Seen from the rear, B. O. could easily be mistaken for a gorilla in clothes. For all this, he remained a gentle soul and a mild mannered curiosity. Never traveling more than fifty miles from home, B. O. eventually began to believe he owned the town. He was not well off but was very proud of a prize pig he possessed. One day he was feeding the pig and discovered a black man having sex with it. The man escaped and B. O., in a colossal rage, pestered every authority figure in town wanting to know if he could kill the man legally if he caught him again. The pig was sold as B. O. considered it contaminated. In his mind all black men were thereafter considered a threat to his pigs. Not receiving a satisfactory answer to his question, B. O. took it upon himself to never let a black man enter his town. Luckily for Axel Fender, his questionable tastes never extended to pigs.

BOSCOE BADASS

Boscoe Badass

Boscoe wasn't nearly as bad after he blew his lower left arm off while dynamiting some stumps. He had very bad eyesight and was almost legally blind. Nonetheless, he drove his old car on all the back gravel roads. Boscoe's favorite passion was to run over varments, as he called them, but could extend to domestic animals, too. Anything smaller than a human was considered "fair game." In the excitement of the chase, he was known to drive into people's yards, etc. No ground was holy. In fact, if you saw him driving anywhere it was considered smart to pull off the road until he was gone as he might run into you by accident. It was common for some people to "bait" Boscoe with fake animals, balls of fur, etc. The perpetrator would hide in a tree with a fishing pole, and cast across the road when he saw Boscoe coming. Seeing a bobbing fur ball crossing the road would get the man every time. The car would chase the thing off the road, across a bar ditch, through a fence and only stop when his car bumper was against the tree. Could the car have climbed trees, he would have pursued the ball of fur into the branches.

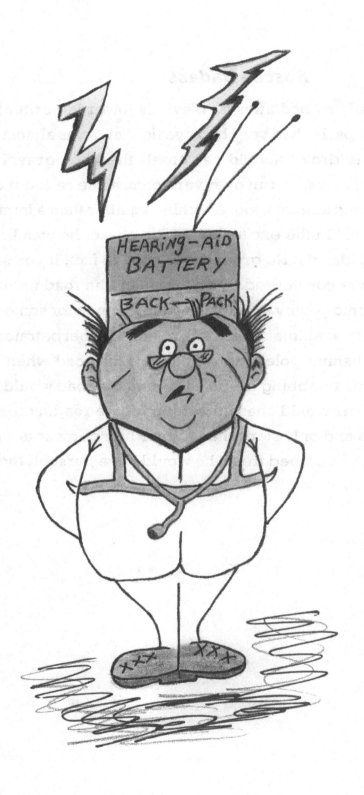

DOCTOR FEELGOOD

Doctor Feelgood

Dr. Feelgood was one of the last of the breed of old time doctors who actually made house calls. He insisted on carrying on his practice well into his nineties. With his failing eyesight, deafness and general forgetfulness, he eventually became as much of a danger to his patients as whatever affliction they suffered from. One of the few higher educated men in town, his humorous quips became well known. When asked if he was going to celebrate his fiftieth wedding anniversary, he answered, "You don't celebrate your mistakes!" As his carelessness grew he often forgot to zip his pants. One of his female patients commented...Dr. you had better close the barn door before the horse gets out! His answer was, "Mildred, the horse has to get up, before it can get out!"

BUNNY GOODBODY

Bunny Goodbody

Goodbody was born the oldest of two children to a pair of brawling alcoholics. Her parent's antics included going after each other to the point of falling to the floor, fighting in public. No other family member looked anything like Goodbody. By fourteen years of age she was at her peak of physical maturity. Her inadequate parents took her to Dr. Feelgood because of this unusual condition where she was declared "overdeveloped" but otherwise physically normal. In a small town, appearance got Goodbody unlimited attention and the world seemed to fall at her feet. She won every beauty contest in the county. Girls wouldn't even enter the contest if they knew she was in it. All this came at no cost in sacrifice, discipline or work. A tendency to rely on looks alone produced a shallow personality. Not particularly smart, Goodbody's mouth was frequently in action without her brain being in gear. Her college career was short lived, as she maxed out twenty-eight credit cards and cost the family their farm. Unable to manage money and with no domestic skills to stabilize a marriage, she was in and out of divorce court, as no man could live with her. She was thoroughly convinced she would be "discovered" by Hollywood even though she had no talent. As an adult, Goodbody was totally self-centered, believing all men should fall to their knees, betray their country and give away real estate if she required it.

BILLY BOB McKNOB

Billy Bob McKnob

McKnob was shooting his pistol on a railroad trestle and was subsequently run over by an Amtrak (they travel at slightly under one hundred mph). He lost one arm and had the other so badly mangled it took over thirty operations to restore it. This left him with no health insurance and hopelessly addicted to pain pills and alcohol. McKnob discovered no one would harm a cripple, no matter what! He moved to a large city where he could annoy <u>more</u> people. Getting arrested was his favorite pastime. Public intoxication was his game. The police eventually would not arrest him because of the verbal hell they endured from him during the time they were forced to keep him. He purchased a cannon which he frequently discharged. During a drinking session he loaded it with <u>gun</u> powder instead of <u>black</u> powder. The resulting explosion tore the cannon to scrap iron. Shrapnel rained down through the trees and a hunk of cannon passed through the neighbor's living room wall between them and the TV. McKnob was miraculously untouched. As his abrasiveness and obnoxiousness increased he began to go to bars where he met other dysfunctionals. Partying with the wrong people, he was abducted by a couple of van traveling perverts. He eventually escaped from them three months later somewhere in New Mexico. A helpless cripple was tailor made for them. McKnob had been repeatedly sodomized and his whole body had been tattooed. This started a revenge fixation whereby he would describe his ordeal to people and implore them to help him find and kill these perverts. These plans also included detailed torture he intended to inflict on his former tormentors.

CASANOVA GOODBODY

Casanova Goodbody

The younger brother of Bunny Goodbody, Casanova ranged from average to sub-standard in just about every way. What he lacked in high IQ, he made up for with his cunning and sneakiness. If he couldn't stop his opponent in football he would use offensive holding or any other illegal action available. Most unusual was his reproductive drive. Having fathered his first child while still in high school, (a stoning offence during the early sixties), he went on to produce twenty-eight children from various marriages. The ones from other sources remain unknown. It was rumored that his alimony payments were being sent to "Occupant." Most of the men in the family liked to drink and fight, especially at public gatherings. Not known to win many fights, they were also notorious wife and girlfriend beaters. If a woman was accidentally killed there was usually a fight at the cemetery between them and the woman's family. However, any family funeral would do. If sufficiently "liquored up" the fight could start early in the church. On one occasion the corpse even became involved in the brawl when the coffin was overturned. Incidents of the father dragging the mother out of a store by the hair of her head, like a caveman, were what Casanova was exposed to as a child. It was common to see him beating hell out of a woman outside a bar at closing time. He totaled at least three cars while fighting women and trying to drive at the same time. Most of these battered women seemed attracted to the behavior, as they usually came back for more.

In the later marriages, Casanova didn't even bother to "Dress Up" for the occasion and had what passed for the reception, at Burger King, or McDonalds. For all of this Casanova may have been the world's second greatest lover. As everyone knows, the world's greatest lover was Fernando Cardova (a little man...but moved like a bandit).

JIMMY THE LOUSE

Jimmy the Louse

Louse should have been the poster child for birth control! A vicious and cowardly, dull-normal human being. This unmanageable boy began beating his parents and locking them out of their own house as soon as he was physically able to do so. He had gone without bathing for so long that fungus grew on him. Louse tried out for the football team but smelled so bad that no one could stand any physical contact. Aside from that, he would "bite" anyone who attempted to block or tackle him. As Louse matured, his sexual behavior took some odd turns for the worse. Mattresses taken from the city dump were stashed all over town for his use. When he was finally "shaken down," mattress wise, they were found from church attics to creek bottoms. His practice was to travel from one mattress to another where he stashed "porno" material and hair spray. He confessed to hair spraying his genitals for the Viagra effect. In a larger neighboring town, Louse joined a dating agency. If unable to get Louse a date the owners would have to return his money. They matched him with a woman so obese she had previously been considered hopeless. After the date the woman stated, "I never want to see him again! I had to go get him because he didn't even have a car. When I asked him what he liked to do, he wanted to know if I had any hair spray." As an adult, Louse became a totally untamed savage whose legacy is too lengthy to be written here.

CRASH

Crash

Crash's claim to fame was an eighteen-inch waist. At almost six feet tall, as she began to fill out, that size waist became an unrealistic burden. One day she was synching down her belt and passed out at the high school. Crash wrecked every car she ever drove, including the drivers education car. She even managed to wreck a car she wasn't even driving. This particular vehicle had a hand accelerator on the column. She left it on to warm up while she was in the house. The vibrations of this caused the shifting arm to jump into reverse. The accelerator must have been cranked up high...as everyone in the house heard a loud "zing," followed by a louder... "pow." The car had shot down the street in reverse and plowed into a parked truck. Crash had her drivers' license revoked in two states. Some people just weren't meant to drive. She moved to California where she obtained a pilots license. Unfortunately, Crash couldn't land a plane and had to be "talked down" twice by a control tower before that license was revoked. Although not as well endowed as Bunny Goodbody, Crash did have a lot of animal magnetism. She eventually married a wealthy attorney, which is good because attorneys need to "catch hell," too!

BOOKWORM

Bookworm

Bookworm wasn't athletically inclined and didn't have any friends, so he spent all his free time reading. The library was his favorite spot. Books took him to places he could never hope to go and opened up whole new worlds for him. One day he found a book on explosives. "Oh, this is fascinating. I can actually make dynamite at home!" During that time you could buy the needed ingredients for dynamite at any drug store. Bookworm mixed his formula and packed it in some two by three inch peanut boxes to cure. One day the family drove to town and he decided, "This is a good time to try out my dynamite." Having only had experience with fireworks, Bookworm had no idea how powerful this amount dynamite was. He lit a fuse giving him time to take cover behind the garage and watched. The dynamite was sitting on the front porch. Said porch vanished in an instant. Lumber, shingles and other debris rained down all over the yard. Every window glass in the entire house imploded causing more damage. When the family came back from town they discovered Bookworm busily trying to nail the porch back on the house. The damage was reasonably noticeable. In later years, when people laugh about such things, his family never did. Bookworm also read books about capturing animals in large straw covered pits. He constructed these pits, but was only successful in capturing outraged family members. That however, is another story.

ANIMAL X

Animal-X

Animal was gifted in so many ways. He matured early and by the time he was thirteen years old he was six feet three inches tall and two hundred and twenty-five pounds. He also was shaving a full beard. His strength would eventually rival that of B. O. Sharp. His father had to weld iron handles in all the tools, axes, etc. because animal was too strong and broke all the wooden ones that he used. He was one of the fastest people on the football team, an incredible thing for a person of his size. Animal could have also become a pornography star, as Mother Nature smiled on him in this department too. Unfortunately he was dyslexic and had difficulty writing anything. During that time dyslexia had no name and people assumed he was mentally lazy. This ruined his college and pro athletic future. Because he never became a predator or used his strength for evil, Animal enjoyed vast popularity and was well thought of. As he further matured physically he developed extremely wide shoulders and a rib cage deep enough to hold a wooden barrel. Those of us near his age who did summer work with him, all knew his physical capabilities. This was not the case with the upper classmen when Animal was a high school freshman. After football practice, Animal was challenged by the strongest senior who already had a scholarship to Oklahoma State. An altercation broke out between the two in the locker room. The perpetrator found himself in a crushing bear hug. After all the air had been squeezed out of the senior, Animal lifted him bodily and shoved him into the overhead plumbing. Animal was never ever challenged again. Additional stories are numerous and varied.

THE CREATURES

The Creatures

The Creature family is reminiscent of what our remote ancestors of one million years ago must have been like. They owned no vehicles, just walked wherever their feet took them; much as the Australian Aborigines do. In the fifties there were a lot of deserted farmhouses in various degrees of collapse. The Creature family would live in one until it fell apart and then move to another. To stay warm at night, they all slept in one room full of corn shucks and also took dogs to bed for additional warmth. If firewood was scarce they would burn parts of the house, starting with the flooring. Hygiene of any sort was unknown! Clothes were only worn for winter, or to go to town. They ate what they could catch in the woods and did not cultivate crops or gardens. If brought one hundred pounds of flour, they immediately made one hundred pounds of bread. Eating what they could and throwing out the rest. People tried to educate the younger ones by taking them to the local school. Unfortunately they didn't understand how they were transported from home to school and when released at the schoolhouse, they returned to the point of pickup and walked to school. The "gap" of transportation was unknown. Eventually they were transported by the school bus and prevented from returning until the bus brought them home. Whereupon they were generally met by naked, hairy, older, adolescent siblings who took them to the house. These younger ones were eventually removed from the parents... a thing unheard of at that time.

If someone out hunting happened to meet the Creatures foraging, they might be tempted to shoot first and ask questions later. Despite their frightening appearance, the Creatures were very benign and almost nonviolent to a fault. On some level they seemed to know they were different from other people. However, if sufficient time was spent in their company, they eventually began to look normal to you. Pictured here is some of the clan. Left to right is Bobcat, Fox, Coyote, and Wolf. Wolf had a bad habit of hiding meat. Fox was always telling him, "It's bad to hide meat—when you dig it up later it can make you sick!" Wolf would respond, "Wolf's teeth are not so good. Hidden meat is more tender and easy to chew." Eventually Wolf would agree not to hide meat, but as soon as no one was looking he would return to his old habit. The whole family wouldn't eat unless their back was to a wall, tree or rock. They feared being attacked from behind and having their meat stolen.

Chapter 2

Animal X and Casanova were the same age and had all their classes together. Also in their class was an individual who had epilepsy. We refer to him as Legion because when Legion "went-off" he had the strength of many. On these occasions it became the "job" of Animal and Casanova to overpower Legion and get an epilepsy pill down him. Animal himself had the strength of at least four and perhaps five. Casanova was to get the pill out of Legion's pocket and was probably chosen for this job because he was so persuasive. A sure sign of a "fit" from Legion was for him to slam both hands down on the desk hard! Ordinary people trying to control Legion during this time had been hurt by him in the past. The whole school became attuned to this standard process and all were familiar with it, especially after eleven or twelve years. Occasionally a new teacher would be employed at the school, but it was rare. Only about one hundred students occupied the high school, and teachers were generally there until retirement. However, a new agriculture teacher was hired to replace the highly revered one of many years who had died. Apparently no one thought to inform him about Legion. Agriculture teachers were always men and were only respected by the all male classes by earning that respect. Not only did the new teacher lack most of his social skills, he also obviously knew nothing about agriculture. As bad luck would have it, on his first day in class Legion "went off." He slammed down both hands on his desk in the middle of the lecture. He then leaped into the air and crashed into a holding area of metal lamps under construction. Pandemonium ensued, Animal and Casanova were on Legion in a flash and the fight was on. Furniture was smashed with people rolling on the floor and others trying to escape. Legion had no fear of being hurt during these times and saw uneven odds against him as just more of an incentive. The new teacher was completely ignored as he shouted, "You boys, you boys, stop that this instant!" Not getting the expected results he continued to threaten and rave. "Stop or I'll have to do something!" Some inner sense must have warned the teacher not to get physical with Animal, because Animal could have popped his head like a grape. Instead he continued to bluster about his authority and position, never realizing

35

the true nature of what was going on. This particular teacher continued to lose all respect from every class until he was finally labeled, "Old C. S." C. S. standing for "Chicken Shit." Jimmy the Louse took it upon himself to be anointed as C. S.'s personal tormentor. The more Jimmy did to C. S. the more cowardly the teacher became.

The Agriculture field trips required students to learn how to do a variety of things. Some of the things with animals included vaccinating, de-horning cattle and castrating hogs, cattle, sheep, etc. While castrating some hogs, Louse saw a way to further agitate C. S. His job was to hold the hog's mouth shut to avoid being bitten and reduce the squealing. Louse decided to stick his fingers in the hog's nose, too; thus suffocating the animal. After the operation C. S. discovered the hog was dead. Most people would have said, O.K. you got some bacon, ham and pork chops in the deal too! C. S. however, panicked - probably in fear of having to pay for the hog. He immediately began to give the hog mouth-to-mouth, attempting to revive it. All he accomplished was to make everyone sick (including the farmer) and his lack of respect hit rock bottom. Not only did Louse make C. S.'s life a living hell at school, he would also attack the man at any time when he was in his vehicle. Jimmy's favorite trick was to play "Chicken" with C. S. He would approach C. S. in the Louse family car head on, at a high rate of speed. C. S. always drove into the ditch to escape. Harassing C. S. became a full time job for Jimmy until old C. S. finally left town in disgrace. The process took almost two years. It was rumored for many years after graduation that Legion had been killed at the state fair. It seemed that he had a "fit" at the midway and a host of people jumped on him and killed him mistaking him for a new ride.

Animal-X eventually married Bunny Goodbody. She was also seeing someone else from another town before they were married. One Day, Animal caught the out-of-towner named Bear at the local Texaco gas station. The out-of-towner, was dragged from his car by Animal and told what would happen to him if he was ever seen by Animal again in that town. Apparently Bear became a believer on the spot. Soon after Animal's marriage he had a family; however, he was suddenly drafted and sent to Viet Nam. During the time he was away, his wife began to "spread her wings," also her legs! She wasn't too particular with the quality or the quantity of her partners. As word of her indiscretions got around, people were appalled at some of her choices, because Animal's wife was something of a "looker." No one wanted to tell Animal about the situation. He was crazy about the woman, and just might "turn on you" rather than accept the truth. After Animal was discharged he returned home to find his wife changed and different. She moved out, got her own place and he didn't know why. Still, no one would tell him. One night he was stalking her new house and discovered the problem. By peeping under her bedroom blinds, Animal saw the worst thing anyone in love can ever see. The man just simply "lost it." He kicked the front door in, grabbed the revolver he had bought for her off the top of the refrigerator and had both of them on their hands and knees begging, naked on the bedroom floor. The man he caught was a bloated toad, nothing at all like Animal. He was all set to pull the trigger and from somewhere in his mind, a voice said to him, "the toad will be dead, you'll be in prison and she will be doing someone else." So Animal went to Bunny's parent's home and told them what he had discovered and asked them, "Now what am I supposed to do?"

For the rest of his life the father could never face Animal. Even when they met on the street, he would look down, or turn away. He must have felt he had failed as a parent. In the divorce, Animal lost child custody, lost his house, lost his car. The Bloated Toad who didn't even own a car was now driving Animals. All he got was a pillowcase with his shaving equipment in it. Animal moved into a broken down trailer house and began to drink and brood. During this time his ex-wife was kicked down the staircase by the Bloated Toad, which caused her to miscarry. The woman was Animal's whole life. He reduced himself to begging her to come back. When she rejected him he found out just how low he had really fallen. During the time Animal was in Viet Nam, some of his friends took measures to attempt to correct Bunny's bad behavior before he got home. One of them said, "My wife is a quality woman, she'll straighten out Bunny." So the quality woman began to hang out with Bunny and they ran around together. Unfortunately, the quality woman became corrupted and was as loose as Bunny. Her husband never found out because the quality woman turned her car over and drowned in a drainage ditch before he could learn of her unfaithfulness. After the divorce, Animal began to drink heavily. One night after he had put away a gallon of vodka and orange juice, he reached the conclusion that life just wasn't worth living. He vowed to take his two tormentors down with him and set out to kill them both. They had moved into a rent house in a nearby town. Animal hid his car and broke in to the house planning to get them when they came home. While he was waiting he found where they kept their alcohol and drank that bottle, too! It became very late and he finally realized that they were not coming home that night. Having his great plan spoiled and also being drunk caused him to go berserk. All the mayhem he had planned for them was visited upon the house. He began in the bathroom by jerking the medicine cabinet out of the wall and slamming it down the commode, breaking the commode into pieces. The sink also followed. He put his fists through walls. He actually jumped up and kicked holes in the ceiling. The couch was run through the living room wall and half of it was sticking out the side of the house. The refrigerator was lifted (still full of food), and thrown into the yard. He broke every window in the place and then finally went home to sober up. The next day the Police were summoned to the scene. Naturally Animal was the No. one suspect. Additionally his fingerprints were everywhere. The Police took lots of eight by ten color photos because they could not believe this was all the work of just one lone individual! You must remember, Animal was not a run of the mill normal human being. He played offensive tackle and defensive end. He was not allowed to rest during the entire game. Always being named all-district, he played with a broken nose, ribs, fingers and broken down arches in his feet. He never missed a game despite these injuries. To their credit and being smarter than they looked, the police phoned Animal instead of going to get him. They were very polite and ask if he would mind coming down to the Police Station sometime at his convenience? That was a bad day for Animal. Not only did he have a nasty hangover, he also discovered the house he had ruined was just a rent house and now he owed a lot of money to a stranger. Or, of course, he could go to jail for a long time. Animal borrowed what he had to as compensation for the damage and went on with his life. It was a good way to put closure on a bad choice. Interestingly enough, Bunny never exhibited the unfaithful sleaziness in high school that she developed as an adult. It was like seeing the playmate of the year seducing every scumbag she met. Animal had to accept the fact that no matter how much you love someone, you cannot change their nature. It just proves the old adage that a good woman can sometimes influence a bad man, but there's not a man on earth that can do anything to change a sorry woman's morals or ambition!

Chapter 3

If Axel Fender was compared to people we know today, the closest character would probably be "The Fonz," characterized on TV's Happy Days played by the actor Henry Winkler. Axel possessed a humorous streak that led to his playing pranks on the unsuspecting. His hot rod had a trap door built into the floorboard. When leaving garages and gas stations, he would drop vital engine parts out the trap door in front of attendants. Pistons, rings, valves, etc. would be left behind in front of astonished onlookers. He would even go to Bandit's garage to perform these acts, even though he never really needed mechanical assistance. One of his best stunts involved placing a small wire cage just behind the radiator. Inside the cage would be the largest wharf rat he could find. The wilder and crazier the rat was, the better. Anyone lifting the car hood would open the trap. He took his car to Bandits garage complaining about a strange noise under the hood. When Bandit raised the hood the wharf rat jumped right in his face and was all over him biting and scratching. Bandit shrieked like an orchestra of scorched cats and immediately beshat himself.

This incident was witnessed by half-a-dozen locals and Axel was banished from Bandits garage until the end of time. Being cast out was no problem for Axel; there were plenty of other victims. He would go to drive-in restaurants with a friend who would pretend to be a deaf mute. When the attendant asks for their order, Axel would go through elaborate sign gestures with the "mute." These gestures would require many minutes to complete. At the conclusion Axel would simply say, "He wants a coke." He installed an iron cage on the back of his flat bed hay truck and convinced one of the Creature family to enter it. The Creature had to promise not to speak, because that would spoil the effect. He also added some loose hay in the floor of the cage and some old bones here and there. Axel collected the order at the drive-in, then the food was tossed into the cage and the Creature fell on it with grunts of satisfaction and loud rejoicing. The drive-in got quiet as a church and peoples eyes bugged out. Axel would continue to terrorize the same drive-ins until eventually no one would wait on him. Axel also expanded into nearby cities where he and two friends would go to a well-to-do restaurant in their suits. At the conclusion of the meal one of them would go into a fake epileptic seizure, falling to the floor, etc. At this point, the other two would rush the afflicted one out to get him some help. In the excitement no one paid the bill. This only worked one time per restaurant. When they got to the last one in town they preformed their act as usual with one extra twist. While the seizure victim was going through all his falling, thrashing behavior, Axel and his other friend got up and left him on the floor still performing. It was a trick, within a trick.

Although Axel was nonaggressive, he would fight back if he felt he was being threatened unreasonably. Axel did not go out for sports yet he was still athletic and strong. He was in the process of a verbal altercation with one of the coaches during a class when the man drew back his fist to hit Axel. With cat quickness, Axel caressed the man's jaw with his "Iron Mike" (his right fist). The coach was out cold! Now Axel found himself in charge of a stunned class. Axel was a man with "Style". He leaned over the unconscious man and made the baseball umpire's gesture for.. "You're Out!" Then he turned to the class and said, "Class dismissed, school's out!". On his way home he stopped by the beauty shop his mother worked at and told her, "I beat up a teacher today". Naturally she dismissed it as one of his jokes, until word began spreading that it was true. Only the fact that the teacher was witnessed preparing to hit Axel, saved him. However, the teaching faculty was hoping he would make one mistake and they were patiently waiting for that moment to expel him. The opportunity came suddenly when Cuban George jumped Axel in the school parking lot. Cuban George was from a nearby air force base and was in his mid twenties. He thought Axel was after his girl friend. Axel later confided, "Cuban George was working me over pretty bad and the teachers were taking their good old easy time doing something about it. "They all wanted to see me get licked and humbled." I got one solid connection on Cuban Georges nose with my Iron Mike and he went down backwards hitting his head on the curb. Now that he was stunned I lit into him with everything I had, before they drug me off him. Cuban George never knew how he was incapacitated. He actually thought I did it." Because he was service personnel and had no business on a school ground, Cuban George got in a lot of trouble over the incident.

When the senior play rolled around Axel decided he wanted a roll in it. Axel was seen as a ruffian and people knew his father and grandfather had done prison time for bank robbery; with his reputation, his attempt to be in the play was discouraged. He and his friend were told they could be stagehands. He took the job and pulled the curtains, etc.

They really should have let Axel in the play because the night before the actual performance he did his thing! The last rehearsal was done and Axel and his friend stayed late and got drunk. Before they locked up for the night they decided it would be very funny to defecate on top of the piano. Which they proceeded to do! The next morning the entire student body was brought into the auditorium to see the senior play. This was the "dress rehearsal" before it was preformed at the P. T. A. the next night.

Axel opened the curtains and sure enough, there was the excrement on the piano, toilet paper and all! At first no one seemed to notice, but then a ripple of excitement spread through the crowd. Soon the entire student body was howling with laughter. Still the teachers had not yet caught on. Finally someone told one of them. "There's shit on the piano!" Axel was told to close the curtain, but he pretended not to hear, as he was in his element.

One of the teachers finally pulled the curtain so that someone could clean the piano. The custodian said, "It's not in my job description." The assistant principal was stuck with the job. Needless to say, this angered him immensely. They tried to continue the play but when the piano player sat down the smell was too much and he kept turning his head, making the most awful faces. All this only served to delight the audience to the point that they became completely out-of-control. Everyone was taken back to class and the principal and assistant principal called in all the known "Bad Asses," of which Axel was one. They said, "Who had the bowel movement on the piano?" Axel responded, "I don't know, but I saw some shit up there." He was told to shut-up! You can go back to that town today and ask any one if they remember what the senior play was about that year and nobody does.

43

However, if you ask them if they remember the violated piano, everyone does!

One semester, Axel's family had to relocate because of his fathers' job. They moved to east L.A., California. Axel found himself in a predominantly Hispanic school. The most popular gang in the school wore long sleeve flannel shirts year round with the top collar buttoned. They also wore do-rags for hats. The girls had a gang too and were known as the "Cho-lo" girls. Their make-up was so thick they looked like circus clowns and the fake eyelashes were several inches long. Axel tried to mind his own business and keep a low profile but it was all in vain. On his first day in school some little "popcorn fart" jumped out from behind a corner and said, "Hey man, give me your lunch money." Trying to be reasonable, Axel articulately responded with "Fuck you!" Suddenly Mexicans came from everywhere. Axel caught the biggest one on the chin with the heel of his hand, being careful not to step on the Mexicans feet at the same time, as this would result in a broken back. Suddenly the Mexicans disappeared like leaves in the wind. It was not to last and Axel, not wanting to kill or maim anyone permanently, discovered that sticks were great equalizers. Axel became a connoisseur of sticks and found the best sticks were springy tree roots that ran along the top of the ground. When extracted from the earth one should try to have a large knob at the business end. At about one ft. long there was plenty of reach, you could carry it concealed and go about your business. Axel had sticks stashed at all emergency locations, his desk, his locker, etc. One day, two other Anglo's moved in and were sent to the same school. All three began to hang together for survival. This only caused larger groups of Mexicans to jump them.

Finally a fight got so big and lopsided it looked like the Alamo. Axel and his two friends were permanently expelled for starting a riot. Interestingly enough, Axel and the other two never started anything. It was simply a matter of people's intolerance for anything different! But what did you expect? Did you think they would expel all the student body except these three? The question of right or wrong did not exist here.

45

Axel's father had taught Axel how to fight though neither was prone to ever start trouble. No one knows where Mr. Fender learned self-defense. It was suspected he picked it up in the service. While Axel's father and grandfather were in prison one of the inmates attacked the old man and Axel's father killed the convict with his hands.

Mr. Fender tattooed himself while in prison. For red coloration he used brick dust. A very tough man! With a marine sergeant's background Mr. Fender ran his household with an iron hand. However, in public he was amiable, retiring and non-assuming.

One night at dinner Axel announced, "I'm eighteen years old now and I bring home some income for this family. I don't like these green beans and I don't think I should have to eat them!" The next thing Axel saw was a big fist that covered his whole face. He and his chair went over backwards and when he got up Mr. Fender said, "Yeah, I've been waiting for this to happen. I heard you won a few fights at school. Just sit your ass down and eat those green beans." About that time Axel's mom started to get up and say something but Mr. Fender added, "You sit down too, unless you want some of the same." Axel noticed little brother shoveling down those green beans. He'd seen what happened to the big boy!

Chapter 4

When Bookworm went into high school he was only five feet tall and weighed one hundred and five pounds. There was an obese upper classman who enjoyed bullying Bookworm. Mr. Pig made Bookworm carry his books, or any other menial thing he could think up. If Bookworm refused, Mr. Pig would use his size and bulk to bully the smaller boy. Tiring of being abused in this way Bookworm appealed to Axel Fender for help. An act in itself that took courage! "How do you plan to fight that four hundred pound tub-of-guts," Axel asked." "I'm up for suggestions," replied the worm. "Well, if you plan to go to fist-city I'd wear some leather gloves for a more compact fist and I'd have a roll of pennies or dimes in each fist. It'll give you twice the punching power. In the meantime you should try to gain some weight and get some serious training done. But I assume you need something more immediate for the near future, right." "That's so," said the worm. Get yourself a lady's long hatpin and run it up your inside sleeve if you're wearing long sleeves. If you're in short sleeves run it down the outside of your pants. The next time Mr. Pig wallows you to the ground get the hat pen out and work him over. Just keep it hidden from him so he won't know how you're doing it. Sure enough, Mr. Pig did his thing on the Worm shortly after that. Mr. Pig got the Worm down and got on top of him. Suddenly Pig began to squeal and holler, "AHHHA! He's sticking me, he's sticking me!" You never saw a fat man move so fast getting off and away from someone. Mr. Pig never bothered the Worm again. Like most bullies he was a coward at heart.

Even a strong man like B. O. Sharp can be taken advantage of if one knows how it's done. B. O. never traveled far from home, but occasionally he liked to go a few miles up the road and across the state line to enjoy a beer at one of the joints that were so prevalent there at the time. Mr. Sharp's physical appearance drew respect, but also envy. On this particular day B. O. was enjoying a cold beer when a motorcycle gang came in the place and began agitating him regarding his appearance. B. O. generally wore his work clothes and looked like a "hayseed." As he tried to leave the place the pack jumped him in the parking lot. Unless B. O. got his hands on someone there wasn't much he could do. He had no fighting skills like Axel Fender

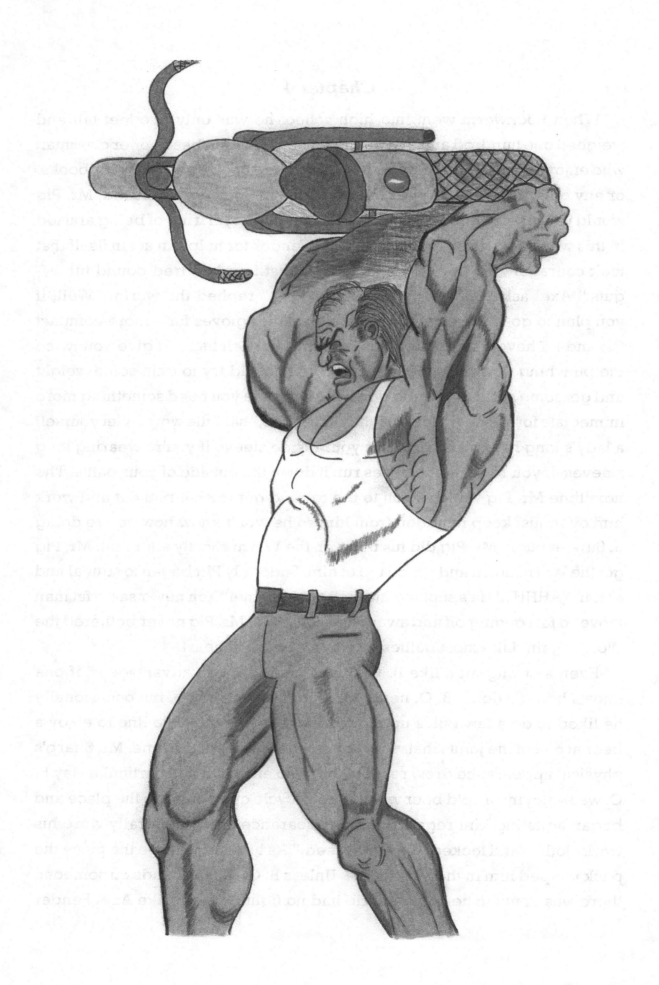

and he did not have the quickness of Animal-X. The pack was cutting him up real bad with their knives and broken beer bottles. It was just a question of time until he passed out from blood loss. In desperation, B. O. grabbed one of the motorcycles and threw it into the group. The kickstand went through one of the packs knee and pinned him to the ground. B. O. got away but took over one hundred fifty stitches from Dr. Feelgood. Feelgood said such blood loss would have killed a lesser man.

Axel Fender and his dad took a trip to New York City in celebration of Axel's graduation. Talk about fish-out-of-water. Axel wore his usual leather jacket, jeans and motorcycle boots. His ex-marine sergeant dad looked even more oddly dressed. Cowboy boots, jeans and western hat marked them as the most noticeable tourists. Especially so with them constantly looking up and gaping at the tall buildings. Suddenly a gang of blacks carrying straight razors surrounded them. The perpetrators moved in close and held a razor to both men's throat as they began cutting their back pockets to get at their wallets. Mr. Fender's background and disposition left him with no fear of death or injury. Axel knew his dad wasn't going to be robbed without a fight, so he was ready when Mr. Fender suddenly without warning yelled, YAAAAH, and grabbed the straight edge by the blade, tore it out of the assailants hand and threw it into the street, along with a gout of blood and gore. The perpetrators weren't ready for what followed at all. Even cut badly the Fenders opened an instant can of "whoop-ass." But it's hard to fight people who are running away. The gang got away with all the Fenders money and they had to wire home for more funds. Mr. Fenders hand was sewn back together but was never completely "right" again. The police were polite but offered little hope of being able to arrest the gang or the return of their money. Of course there was always danger at home. One does not have to travel to New York City to find it. Firewater Barstool, in one of his lucid moments, heard a noise outside his house he shared with his mother. Upon peeping out the window he discovered Catshit Looney busily mowing their yard. Catshit would mow people's yard without being asked, even if it didn't need mowing just to get money. He would even mow your yard with snow on the ground. If you couldn't pay he would fall upon you and hurt you with righteous vengeance and sometimes molest you in the process, depending on his mood and what he thought he could get away with! No one ever willingly let him in their house. "That knuckle dragging son-of-a bitch is mowing our yard again Ma." "What'll we do son?" "Got anything in your purse or the cookie jar? If so, we'll just slip it out the mail slot in the door when he gets done." "And if we don't have enough, what then?" "Then we may get to know him intimately." "Maybe we could slip out the back and make a run for it." "No Ma, if he catches us in the open we're goners. Damn, he's more persistent than the Jehovah's Witnesses!"

Occasionally Catshit would get a job at the local rodeo when it was in season. He and B. O. Sharp would work the stock in the back and get them ready to release. B. O. had no fear of Catshit as he could turn him any way but loose if the occasion arose. Neither man was overly "bright" and one day they left the communication speaker on after talking with the announcer. Out of nowhere and without warning, their voices in argument were suddenly broadcast all over the arena. "God damn you, Catshit!" "Fuck you, B. O.!" They were not asked to work the rodeo again.

Every new preacher who came to town was obsessed with saving the abundant supply of weirdoes. The Baptist church had just installed a new baptistry behind the pulpit with a plexiglass front. One night they persuaded Catshit to be baptized. The organ was playing softly, the choir was doing background and the lights were low. All attention was on the preacher and Catshit. The preacher made all the appropriate comments and immersed Catshit. Upon being drawn out of the water, Catshit shouted, "God damn that waters cold!"

On more than one occasion Catshit had been discovered masturbating to Bandit Hangings porno material. People tolerated it as long as it wasn't too blatant. But, when he was caught in the act by one of the towns leading citizens in his rent house things began to happen. Catshit was sent to Dr. Feelgood where he confessed to masturbating nine to ten times a day. The Dr. said, "Mr. Looney, nine to ten times a day is highly excessive. Man, you've got to get a-hold of yourself." Catshit said, "I do Dr., nine or ten times a day." Being the closest thing the town had to a psychiatrist, Dr.

Feelgood ask Catshit, "Is your mother a nagger?" Catshit responded, "No, she's a white woman!" "You're sure she's not a nagger?" "No, god-damnit I already told you, she's a white woman." Catshit was diagnosed as being chronically "jack batty."

The next day Dr. Feelgood found Ruff Brier collapsed in his office. "What seems to be the problem, Ms. Brier?" "Dr. I'm hurt! That god-damn man friend of mine was in from the army and nearly fudged me to death!" "Fudge? Oh! You mean carnal knowledge?" "Nah, he's not a Catholic." "Well, how long was his furlough?" "About eleven inches I guess!" "No, no, I mean how long was he off?" "Oh, just long enough to piss!" "I'm placing you in the charity ward of the hospital for observation."

While Ruff was hospitalized, the doctor prescribed some drugs that had a negative side affect on her. She was reduced to the level of an animal (not such a long trip). The woman was like an ape at the zoo. If anyone came in the room she would shit in her hand and throw it at them. The hospital staff kept a trash can lid (the round metal kind) near the door to use as a shield if they had to go in. It was Ruff's only trip to the hospital.

Dr. Feelgood's hearing and eyesight continued to deteriorate after he passed into his 90's. If he forgot his glasses and went to town it was common for him to mistake inanimate objects for people. He would speak to mail boxes and trash cans. He stomped a man's foot and dumped his cigar ash in the man's mouth when the man opened up to scream. "Oh! Sorry sir, I thought you were an ash can."

When Dr. Feelgood was younger he planned a fishing trip to Mexico. Unfortunately, he had to have emergency back surgery shortly before the trip. Not wanting to lose the trip that was paid for in advance, he went anyway, even though he was confined to a wheelchair. When the plane arrived in Mexico, there was no way to wheel yourself off like you could in the states. Instead, a very tall staircase was wheeled out on the runway for deplaning. The staircase was too narrow for the wheelchair, so two Mexicans lifted the terrified doctor in the chair overhead and walked down with the chair tilting from side to side at precarious angles. They then threw him into the floor of a bus, like cordwood, while they tied the wheelchair to the bus roof. The good Dr. had to lay with the luggage and try to avoid the chickens and small pigs running loose at random in the bus floor. They did not collapse the chair on the bus roof. It was bungee cord tied in an upright position. He could hear tree limbs and phone wires slapping it as they drove and he was thinking, "That chair is my only transportation." The travel agent had assured him that everything in the town would be handicapped equipped. Well, nothing was! The rest room doors were too narrow for his chair to fit through, so the hotel gave him the penthouse suite. The first day he found out that spokes fly out of wheels when you have to roll over cobblestone streets. This resulted in a flat tire. It literally took an act of God to get a wheelchair flat fixed.

The next day he went deep sea fishing with the other tourists. They were after the big tarpons and large sail fish. These large fish put up a great fight and are hard to land. Because of the size of these fish, everyone is seat belted in their chair. Unfortunately the seat belt would not fit around the wheelchair, so Feelgood did without one! He got a big fish on his line right away and shot out of the seat and slid down the deck on his side, busily trying to reel in the fish all the while. The crew managed to capture him before he went off the end of the boat, but they were not happy. If not fishing, life was fairly dull in the town.

One day at the market he saw some very attractive women. Upon inquiring about them he was told that they were from the whore house. Whore House!!! Well you never saw a wheelchair move so fast. When he arrived at the destination it was discovered that the whore house was on the third floor. No ramps—just stairs! People offered to carry him into the whore house but he refused. I don't mind being carried out of a whore house but I'll be dammed if I'll be carried in to one. The situation was like a one-eyed cat peeping into a seafood shop window. Hopeless! Feelgood's wife of many years had begun to deteriorate mentally shortly after their marriage. In the fullness of time she became a bitch-on-wheels, a chainsaw-in-a-skirt! The Dr. eventually loathed her so badly he divorced her. The day he fell off the roof of his house, causing the back surgery, he remembered thinking, "this is it, I'm dead now." When he regained consciousness in the hospital she was his first sight leaning over him. He said, "Good lord, I'm in hell!!"

Chapter 5

After the incident involving the brutal cutting of B. O. Sharp, Casanova, his friends and family decided to retaliate on the pack. There's no way to know if they felt loyalty to B. O., or if they thought their town needed avenging, or if it was just a good excuse to fight someone. It could be some of all three! Casanova and his family did love to fight. Anyway you preferred they would try to accommodate you, fists, knives, chains, etc! They did not use guns, as that tended to kill you permanently. During B. O.'s incapacity they went across the state line in massive numbers to the sight of the incident. The atmosphere was festive much like a rival football game. The mob descended upon the bar where the pack hung-out and waited. All the tables were pushed together in a half circle facing the door, and in many layers deep. As the evening progressed and no pack members appeared they began to get drunk and loudly make fun of everyone entering the bar. Someone would come in and suddenly they were "on stage." A perpetrator from the audience would shout, "Look at that guy, the only thing going through his head is lice." The entire place would rock with laughter. No one did anything about this, what would they do? They couldn't fight everyone in the bar. As nothing came of all this everyone eventually went home with high spirits and high from spirits.

What Casanova's family considered a vacation was to travel to the nearest metroplex for gang warfare. There was an established place where people met to fight. No matter how you wanted to fight or with any weapon of choice there was always someone there who would accommodate you. A good deal of betting also went on regarding the outcome of each altercation. The building where all this occurred was a hard-core weight lifting gym. After work hours the owner closed the business and opened for "fight night," as the house took a percentage of the betting. Casanova was broken from this particular recreation when some worthy foe imbedded an ice pick in his shoulder. The ice pick penetrated the bone with such force that it required several people just to pull it out. Thereafter Casanova confined his fighting to the bush leagues.

Not only was the man a compulsive rowdy, he also was an incurable womanizer. After a certain number of divorces Casanova was looked upon as a public nuisance. He was eventually forced to attain marriage licenses in other states. Divorces didn't bother him as he was financially picked clean of all money and possessions by this process long ago! The amount of social infections and cases of body lice he acquired over the years is anyone's guess. One night he was busily performing with his newest acquaintance when she began to jerk and vibrate all over. Casanova thought, "man, I'm really good at this." Unfortunately the woman was having a seizure. This turned even Casanova off when he realized what was actually going on. Repeated attempts at this always brought these seizures on and he was forced to abandon his efforts at this activity. The only similar occurrence in this arena was his experience with a small Asian woman. The thrashing and violent jerking was doing his ego no end of good until he discovered he had accidentally forced her head between the headboard of the bed and the mattress, thus causing near suffocation. His worst two disasters occurred in rapid succession on the same weekend. The first was on a Saturday night. Every time the woman "got off" she would urinate on him. If nothing else, this was a bad distraction. She tried to pass it off as sweating, but Casanova knew better. Hoping for better luck on Sunday night with another beady-eyed prospect, he proceeded to do his thing. Everything was going well until he began to smell something really bad! Further investigation revealed that this one had crapped all over them both and his bed too. Casanova swore off sex for an entire week and bought rubber sheets.

In his senior years, Casanova obtained a license to work as a massage therapist. This occupation turned out to be a disaster. I mean, would you hire a fox as a security guard for your chicken house? His license was revoked for massaging women on body parts that were considered class three misdemeanors to touch. It appears that the business wasn't all that successful anyway. Because Casanova had given out an excessive amount of free treatment passes. It is interesting to note the word therapist breaks down to spell: "the rapist."

Everyone knew how awful Boscoe Bad Asses eyesight was. Considered almost legally blind, he was an outright peril to all who came in contact with him. The town he lived in had no police, so if anyone needed police assistance they were forced to phone the nearest Sheriff. Boscoe did not own a phone and had to go some distance to find a pay phone. He had phoned the police department repeatedly regarding a reoccurring problem. The nature of his complaints were rarely taken seriously because he always reported that men from Mars were in his house, pissing on him. Eventually the Sheriff's department made this house call even though they felt it would be a long trip for nothing. Arriving at Boscoe's residence they found a partially collapsed wood frame house. The only thing still supporting the structure was most likely "termites holding hands." Half way through the house the police were forced to crawl through a hallway where the roof had collapsed to within a few feet of the floor. The flooring at that point had rotted away and the police were proceeding on hands and knees through a dirt floor. Finally arriving at Boscoe's bedroom, they were able to stand upright again. "There they are," shouted Boscoe. Those bastards are pissing on us right now! The men from Mars were in fact two young boys who had climbed into the overhead beams and were shooting them with water guns.

Most everyone feared what might happen if Boscoe and Crash ever met in motorized transportation of any kind. Boscoe was blind as a bat and everyone avoided him on the roads. Crash was a woman of notoriety who probably should just avoid all mechanical contrivances, forever. Crash had previously wrecked the driver's education car by plowing into a bridge abutment, having nearly missed the bridge entirely. Incredibly, she was never ever physically injured. The two of them met one icy winter day in traffic but not in a manner you would ever suspect. A long line of traffic was stalled behind a car that could not negotiate a slight rise at a stop sign. The problem car's wheels would spin on the ice but no traction kept it immobile. Crash was the last person in the line of cars. She happened to glance in her rear-view mirror and was horrified to see Boscoe approaching, "hell-bent-for-leather" at a speed impossible to stop short of an impact. Crash panicked and jumped from the doomed vehicle. She slipped, fell on her ass and slid into a near-by ditch. Boscoe smashed into the rear of her car causing a chain reaction. All the cars buckled like an enormous train derailment and the lead car shot across the intersection like a bullet. A policeman eventually arrived and gave all involved parties a ticket for hitting the person ahead of them from behind. When he approached Crash she protested that this was not right because she had not actually been in the car at all during the wrecks. She still received a citation for leaving the scene of an accident.

Crash's driver's education days were a nightmare for everyone involved. No students wanted to ride with her and the principal aged visibly, as he had to ride and supervise her. The principal always had her drive on back country gravel roads. There was less chance of her meeting someone there that she might run into. On this particular day Crash was driving with an accompaniment of terrified students and a nervous principal on Valium. On a lonely back road they approached a parked car blocking half of the road. The principal instructed Crash to go around the vehicle slowly. As they crept around the car they discovered a squatting woman urinating. The principal shouted, "Go back, go back." Never, never shout at Crash during moments of stress. She will always do the unexpected and usually the worse thing possible. Crash panicked and the car leaped forward knocking the pissing woman aside. They never went back, all things considered. However, the incident was not to be forgotten and people talk about it to this day.

Bookworm had the "hots" for Crash but would never act on the fact as he had a low self-image and could not stand the thought of her rejecting him. He settled for secretly admiring her and fantasizing. Their class had a lake party one year and both of them were in attendance. Unfortunately there was no rest room facility in sight when nature began to call Bookworm. One can only put certain things off for so long. Finally in desperation Bookworm reasoned, "I'll just go in the lake and no one will be the wiser." Finding a rather secluded spot Bookworm waded out about waist deep and lowered himself down facing the beach. Of all times for Crash to pick to talk to Bookworm, it had to be at that moment. As she approached Bookworm he looked like a trapped animal. He figured, "If I lean back maybe it'll go

56

behind me." Unfortunately just the opposite happened. As soon as Crash arrived a steaming turd popped up between them. What are you going to do? Blame it on the fish! Crash beat a hasty retreat and Bookworm said to himself, "well, I can forget about ever asking her out!"

Crash got a job working as a hostess for a local restaurant. One night was especially crowded with customers when the Creature clan dropped by to collect any garbage the restaurant didn't want. Not realizing that the intercom was on and that she was right on top of it, Crash announced, "look everyone, it's the Clampits." All eyes went to the Creatures in the doorway. This is an example of an awkward moment reaching "critical mass."

The amazing thing about the Creature family is that they could survive if civilization collapsed, whereas ordinary man probably could not. They understood that willow bark was the key ingredient in aspirin. They could eat all manner of grubs and grasshoppers that modern man would hesitate to touch. They knew cattail roots and wild onions could be dug up with sticks. All these things and more are available when game is scarce. As Crocodile Dundee once said, "It tastes like shit, but you can live on it."

One cold winter day one of the Creatures stopped by the store to borrow some fire. It seems that their fire had gone out at home and they needed a live coal to get it going again. Curious to see how this could be accomplished, onlookers watched the Creature take a handful of cold ashes and work a hot coal out of the fire into his palm of ash. He then took off for home with no pain. Everyone learned something that day.

The Creatures seemed impervious to infections and ailments you would expect from their filthy living and lack of hygiene. The town's first septic system emptied into what we called the sewer ponds...two black lakes of pure filth. Adolescent boys would go there to watch the prophylactics float to the surface and fanaticize. One day a Creature family member killed a coot there. Coots are a relative of the duck family and not considered eatable. The coot fell in the sewer pond after being hit with a rock. The pond was almost vicious enough to walk on. In spite of all this, the Creature swam out and retrieved his meal.

Chapter 6

Billy Bob McKnob was always bad, but after he lost an arm, his behavior went completely over the top. Before his accident he would go drinking and driving in his convertible. Going down the highway he would throw empty beer bottles straight up in the air, (if the top was down), and just drive out from under them. This only worked well if you were not being followed closely by another vehicle.

No one would hire him for farm work because McKnob had no patience and liked to get things done "quickly." He promptly destroyed all farm equipment that he touched. Plowing, for example has to be done in first gear as the discs are set deeply into the ground, (as deep as one foot). The soil is then lifted and turned outward at approximately ten inches in height. McKnob was observed plowing from a nearby road and, on this particular occasion, he had somehow managed to get the tractor into road gear, an almost impossible accomplishment while pulling a plow. A rooster-tail of dirt was flying behind the plow as high as a house, and the discs couldn't have been more than an inch deep in the ground. The job was quickly done, but the field was not properly plowed. The equipment was also badly damaged. He decided on one occasion that a certain gravel road didn't need to be where it was and he simply plowed across the road making it part of the field. It was later explained to him that this was not his decision since the transportation system of county and state outranked his ideas. That section of road had to be completely reestablished at some cost to taxpayers.

After his accident he deteriorated noticeably, as no one could do anything about his behavior. It seems that no matter how deranged and psychotic someone is, people are reluctant to hit a cripple. You couldn't go out to eat with him as he would scratch his scrotum with the silverware, or lewdly expose himself in the serving line while waiting to eat. If he saw someone headed for the drinking fountain he might rub his genitals on the spigot right in front of them.

He really enjoyed standing at the top of stairs when people were ascending toward him. When they were close enough he would urinate on the top steps thoroughly splashing everyone. He was eventually hired to work in a gun store and he made some slight effort to clean up his act. One particular day he was attempting to fix a lawn mower in the gun shop. He started the mower in the shop, forgetting that it was wall-to-wall carpet. The rug got caught in the blades and, before it could be deactivated, a huge hole had been carved out of the carpet while the mower ran-amuck throughout the shop. Dust flew thick and customers fled in all directions.

While working in the gun shop McKnob came across a very cheap handgun they carried among their inventory. It was mostly plastic and, as a result, would melt if over fifty rounds were fired through it. Although the owner disliked selling this merchandise it was necessary to buy this product in a package deal in order to obtain the quality guns he needed at a discount price. From the looks of the people who purchased this weapon, it was fairly clear what their intentions were. It was basically a "Saturday night special" primarily used to rob 7-11 stores and other such likely places. With the owners permission, McKnob loaded a box of ammo extremely "hot", to be given with each purchase of this particular revolver, absolutely "free." As the trigger was pulled on this gun, with this ammo, the potential for the gun exploding in the users' hand was high. (Who knows, maybe this was a blessing in disguise.)

The owner of the shop was an ex-Viet Nam vet who was a demolition expert. He liked war and changed his name in an attempt to do a fourth term in Nam. He would parachute into China, blow up air bases and then walk back to Nam. The man never really adjusted to civilian life. He owned eight machine guns and was never far away from at least one of them. At this time, he had no arrest record at all. However, he began to use drugs. When some debtors (who owed him a considerable sum of money) refused to pay him, he tortured and killed them. At present he is doing life without parole and the gun shop remains closed.

McKnob's brief attempt to reform his behavior failed miserably and he went back to being his unbearable self. However, the man could be clever if the situation demanded it. As he was out driving one night with a female companion, he failed to stop at a stop sign. This was witnessed by a police

60

vehicle and McKnob was pulled over. Thinking quickly, he ran back to the officer and said, "I'm sorry officer for running that stop sign, but that little girl with me bit me on the end of my dick and I just couldn't help myself." The policeman became so amused at the idea he lost all composure and told McKnob to just go!

When McKnob was drunk-or-high, which was often, he developed the very bad habit of masturbating in front of people. He was eventually cured of this behavior by one of the Creature family. Not that the Creatures had any problem with nudity, they routinely went naked at home, or while foraging for food. They did know you had to wear something if you went to town and they therefore knew McKnob's behavior was wrong. On this eventful day when McKnob "whipped it out" in public, the Creature grabbed it and ran off with it. McKnob, not wanting to lose his parts and being literally and figuratively attached to that appendage was obliged to run off too! A very painful experience! He never exposed himself around the Creatures again.

The Creature family had an unusual waste disposal system at home. It was similar to the ancient Vikings system. They owned no outhouse, no plumbing of any sort and yet they devised the following plan: They dug a pit and placed a log at the edge of it. One simply hung off the side of the log over the pit. In time the pit was covered with dirt and the log was rolled to another spot, with a new pit. All went well unless you lost your balance and fell backward into the pit. If this occurred it was a cause of much revelry. Almost to the point of declaring a holiday. They had no TV and obviously didn't get out much!

Other than the Creatures, the only other "pit digger" in town was Bookworm. He had read about capturing animals in the tropics with pits. One day he found an army shovel in the garage for digging "fox holes." "This is just what I need to dig my pit," he thought! Their forty acre wheat field had been recently cut (but not by McKnob) and this was where the pit was created. After about four feet of digging the pit became larger as a means of preventing prey from escaping. The dirt was scattered and wheat straw was placed over the hole. No bait was used. It was just a random hole that depended on luck and the un-wary.

The next day his mother woke him for breakfast and said, "Your dad was sure mad at you this morning." Worm said, "What did I do now?" Did you dig a hole in the field? Well, yes! Your dad fell in it today!

The father had a horrible temper and Worm dreaded that evening when he would get off work. At suppertime Worm was upstairs hiding under the bed. "Come and eat," they said. "He won't hurt you." "No," said the Worm, "it's a trick!" His mother then ran him out from under the bed with a broom handle, amid "dust bunnies" and such, all in his hair. "Well, I'm not going to whip you," his dad said. "Did you fall on your <u>head</u>?" the Worm asked! No, I didn't.

Worm's dad, Casey, commuted to work via car pool. The pool arrived at his house just as the drama unfolded. All Casey's work buddies witnessed the man running across the field to capture some cows that had escaped.

Suddenly he disappeared into a hole. He just vanished. Climbing out of the pit he was heard to comment "To hell with those cows." He limped back to the waiting car and headed for work where he heard all kinds of ha ha's and ho ho's.

Someone said they might buy Worm a shovel for Christmas. Another mentioned that he might get Casey a long stick to poke around the ground when he went outside of his house. Others said Casey was religiously living near holy ground. By days end at work even Casey was laughing at the mornings happening.

On his arrival home Casey relented about further punishment for his "hole-digging son." However, he was most adamant about planning Worms's evening for him. As he told him to get his ass outside post haste and fill in every hole.

Chapter 7

Jimmy the Louse was not the only bad apple on his family tree. His maternal grandmother, old lady McSwindell, was an embarrassment to the whole town. Her game was suing everyone in sight. She was particularly aggressive toward the bus and transportation companies. She tried to enter a bus one day with her dog. The driver told her, "I'm sorry lady; the bus company forbids animal transportation." She got angry and told the bus driver, "You know where you can stick this bus." He replied, "Well, if you do the same thing with the dog, you can <u>ride</u> on the bus."

Thereafter, Mrs. McSwindell would fake a serious fall on every bus she rode on and threaten to sue, or settle out of court. She became so notorious for this that both national bus companies had her picture posted for all drivers to <u>never</u> allow this woman to enter a bus.

Jimmy stunk so bad that one of his teachers decided to do a home visit. It was raining on the day Ms. Duright dropped by the Louse house. After being invited in she propped her yellow umbrella against a wall and noticed a lot of black spots going up it. Then to her horror, she saw the same thing happening to her legs. Busily brushing off both legs, she announced, "You people have fleas." The Louse family just sat there scratching and replied, "We know it." As soon as Ms. Duright sat down in one of the padded chairs a host of roaches swarmed over her legs and lap. After looking around, she was further appalled to see little piles of dog droppings on the carpet. Cats occupied the upper levels of the house, tops of sofas, cabinets, chairs or anywhere out of the reach of the dogs. Dogs of course ruled the floor area. There weren't just a few cats, there were scores of them. An educated guess would approximate close to one hundred cats in the house.

Duright said, "I came here to discuss Jimmy's problem, but now that I've arrived I believe I know what it is. You people have got to get rid of some of these cats." The Louse family looked shocked and said, "But we love our kitties." In the middle of the interview, Ms. Louse suddenly jumped up and ran out of the room. There was no explanation, no I'll be right back, no nothing. She was just gone.

In her absence Ms. Duright thought, "I guess she will be back eventually." While waiting, she began to notice the shimmering wallpaper and thought it might be iridescent. However, closer examination proved to be roaches all over the walls. When Ms. Louse finally returned, (with no explanation for her absence), she was asked to sign a paper for the teacher, proving she had done her home investigation. Upon getting a pen out of her pocket, Duright discovered a tiny little roach on the tip of her pen. She just flicked it off and felt it was no big deal at this point. Duright thought she had smelled something earlier when she drove up in front of the Louse house. Now she knew it was the house itself which could be smelled for some distance. Duright did not go back to school that day. Instead she went home and took a bath in a tub of strong cleanser.

As Jimmy matured, it was obvious that he was developing a condition which was rapidly causing him to become a hunchback. This condition caused him to have to buy larger shirts. Axel Fender used to say, "He's so hunchbacked he has to take off his shirt just to shit!"

Louse also became over weight. Now you have an overweight hunchback who wants to join the gymnastics team at school. Since it wasn't a contact sport no one objected. Louse wasn't very good but he kept at it. Eventually there was a gymnastics tournament. About the only event Louse was good at was a movement on the high bar known a "belly grinds." One simply leaned over the bar at waist level and used both hands on the bar to propel you around and back to your original position in a headfirst manner. Since there was some flex in the bar, momentum could be utilized to build up some speed. This really worked well if the subject was overweight, which tended to make Louse a natural for this event.

When it was his turn to perform he got his belly grinds going so fast his body became just a blur. Because he was overweight Louse didn't wear traditional gym attire. He had on instead, a pair of rubber stretch shorts. During the course of this frantic activity, the top of his shorts became overlapped on the bar. He was traveling at such a fantastic speed that the shorts shrunk up in an instant. They drew up inside the crack of his ass until they disappeared. Somehow in this process, his testicles also lapped over the bar. Now Louse jerked to a sudden stop and let go of the bar hanging upside down screaming, "my balls, my balls." The officials tried to unwind him but it was to no avail. During the excitement the audience left the seats and crowded around offering advice. All the while Louse is screaming about his testicular problem. Finally one of the judges got out his pocketknife and began to trim the rubber shorts off of Jimmy. Louse became frantic and shouted, "Don't cut my balls off." There was a little girl standing nearby who pulled on her mothers dress and asked, "Mama, what are balls?"

A similar incident happened in the home of Bandit Hanging. However, there was less sympathy for him than Jimmy the Louse. On this particular day, Bandit was upstairs preparing to take a bath. He was just about to get in the shower when his wife began bitching about the sink leaking in that bathroom. Knowing if he didn't fix it promptly he wouldn't "get any" that night, Bandit went right to work. Working on a sink naked would be safe in most houses, except this house had a large yellow tomcat. Bandit was down on his hands and knees fixing the pipes and was unaware of the cat behind him.

Cats are fascinated by moving objects and this cat was no exception. The cat sat there watching those balls swing back and forth and knew he couldn't live another day without them. Suddenly the cat moved forward and snatched the object of his fascination with both front feet, claws extended. Bandit screamed and jumped up. However, he was still under the sink and knocked himself out when his head came in contact with the sink bottom. His wife hearing the commotion rushed upstairs to discover an unconscious naked man in the floor. She promptly phoned an ambulance.

Upon arriving, the paramedics were just in time for Bandit to begin regaining consciousness. They loaded him on the stretcher and were negotiating their way carefully down the stairs. All the while Bandit was telling them what happened, and how it was all the fault of that damn cat. Both paramedics laughed so hard that they accidentally dropped Bandit off the stretcher. He continued to fall the remainder of the way down the stairs. He suffered, not only a concussion, but a broken leg, as well. The story of the scratched nuts and other assorted injuries got all over town and was the most talked about event at the hospital. This particular incident was passed from hospital to hospital and has previously appeared in print at least one other time.

Smaller tragedies in Briar Patch occurred every time Firewater Barstool (the barber) cut someone's hair. Because he was usually in some state of intoxication, Firewater would clutch you and lean on you in order to remain upright while he worked.

One day he cut Axel Fenders hair. Being an Elvis impersonator, Axel was particular about his hair. Unfortunately, Firewater got one sideburn two inches higher than the other one. Axel noticed that he was being butchered and said, "stop, that's just how I want it." He immediately drove to another town where a real barber attempted to salvage the damage. It was Axels first and last trip to Firewater's place.

Most of Barstool's regular customers were truck drivers passing through town that saw his roadside shop and just didn't know any better. Occasionally Firewater would hallucinate and chase the ever popular "little green men" about the shop. Those who witnessed this behavior never returned to his shop and no one ever let him shave them with a straight razor.

Someone once commented that Barstool wore the worst looking hair piece that they had ever seen. It was described as looking like a dead cat curled up on top of his head. They were informed that it was not a wig. It turned out that he cut his own hair and the back was particularly hard to do even with the help of mirrors.

Barstool and his mother lived two blocks from the volunteer fire department. One evening they were sitting on the front porch when the town fire alarm went off. This was a big deal in Briar Patch, as there was a serious absence of excitement locally. Both he and his mother got up to watch the local businessmen rush to the fire station. The truck pulled out and his mother commented, "Their headed this way." Then she said, "their getting closer." Sure enough they were headed to the Barstool house which was in fact in the process of burning up while these two sat on the porch completely unaware. Firewater had been burning trash in the backyard and apparently smoldering papers had landed on the roof.

Chapter 8

Animal-X never really recovered from Bunny's bad behavior. It took years for him to overcome the pain and loss. He almost lost the right to see his son because of his anger over the situation. Animal would go to what used to be his house to pick up the boy and there was always a verbal exchange between him and Bunny. Her "significant other" was smart enough to keep quiet and stay uninvolved. This became so bad that Animal had to have counseling which involved the following:

Say, "I'm here to pick up the boy." Don't go in the house, don't say anything else! Also he was instructed to remove the tomb stone from his living room. The granite marker had Bunny's date of birth and date that she divorced him. This was having a bad effect on the child.

Their basic problem stemmed from their differing belief system. Animal felt that sex was an act of love and a sacred thing between married couples. Bunny, however, saw it as a bodily function that happen to feel good. It was no more significant to her than eating a cookie. She began to frequent the truck stop at the edge of town. It was common to see her bringing home truckers, two and three at a time. Bunny became known at the truck stop as the "Road Whore".

Before Animal married Bunny she had no sexual past. This was not unusual for a small town in that era. There was no way to know she would abandon her traditional upbringing so completely and so vividly.

However, as time passed, Animal seemed to accept the situation. Just when it seemed that he had adapted his thinking on her current behavior, Bunny came back into his life.

She began to show up at the restaurant where he ate lunch. At first she wanted to borrow some money. Animal agreed but he did not think she would pay him back. If she did not reimburse him, she wouldn't be able to face him and he wouldn't have to see her again, he reasoned. Unfortunately, she did pay him back the next week and began to drop by at lunch frequently. Animal said Bunny was no damn good and he had his guard up. He was determined not to let her get to him. But as time passed she continued to show up. She was nice to him and seemed to know just what to say and do. All the original magnetism that made their relationship special was there to tap into. Likely it always would be. Before too long they were seeing each other again. However, Bunny might disappear at any time from three days to three weeks.

Animal became frustrated with her behavior and he asked her "What <u>am</u> I to you?" She would reply, "Why, you are my very best friend" and also add, "I don't care if you sleep with other women." Animal said, "I can't be involved with you sexually and emotionally and want other women too. I come to you looking for some human warmth and compassion and worst of all, I have to explain this to you." Bunny would say, "You place too much value on sex." "No", Animal said, "You don't place enough value on it. You stomp all over our marriage vows and venerated traditions without so much as a by-your-leave, as if they were so much dog shit! As soon as my back is turned you behave like an unleashed yard dog. I don't know why you act like a two dollar strumpet, but since I can't save you from yourself, the only equation left may be to save <u>me</u> from <u>you</u>!"

Animal was reluctant to give up on Bunny. After all, she had given him her innocence. This was very important to him because you could only do it once.

One day Animal overheard a phone conversation between Bunny and one of her girlfriends. Bunny said, "No one is going to tell me who to fuck! If I want to fuck someone, I will!" After overhearing this, Animal realized Bunny was telling him whatever she needed to—to get herself through certain moments.

Because she was so unstable, her behavior caused Animal to become insecure. This was a new and alien sensation to him. He began to leave his job in the middle of the work day to check on her. She became his obsession.

One day he left work to drive by her place. Sure enough, there was a collection of strange vehicles at the residence. Knowing the worst was going on, Animal, at this point, was past reasonable thinking. He kicked the front door off the wall. At the sight of him, men scattered in all directions.

Some went out windows still clutching their clothes. Animal disrobed and took their place telling Bunny, "But I <u>really</u> love you!"

The next day he went to a psychiatrist. This was a necessity because he might well have committed murder at some point. Animal would not only have killed someone but maybe himself too!

Some hard facts came out of his psychiatric sessions. According to the doctor, Bunny was a loser from the family of losers. She might be the "pick of the litter," but was quite dysfunctional. The doctor further said, "If she was a car she would need an entire motor, transmission overhaul, not just a spark plug change". A person like Bunny does not realize her behavior is wrong. Thus, they rarely seek professional help. If, however, they become traumatized they will seek temporary help; but only until the trauma passes. A person with Bunny's problems might need counseling possibly for a lifetime, but they often never received it. Therefore, Bunny might continue her perversions indefinitely.

Animal soon realized that you couldn't make someone like Bunny any more normal by simply having good sex. This observation applies no matter how gifted her partner was, or how well they performed.

Animal figured that if God made anything better than a good woman, he kept it for himself!

The abundance of religious zealots caused Briar Patch to be a very boring town. It had to close the billiards parlor and the movie house because they were considered sinful. It seemed that people had nothing better to do than sit around and speculate whether or not old man Smith was a secret hermaphrodite. This was alleviated somewhat by people like Axel Fender, a natural born prankster.

Axel had recently given up fornicating with cattle and had turned to women. As he had good transportation, he could go to other towns where his family was unknown. This enabled him to start a normal and new life. When asked why he gave up cattle, his response was, "Nine of ten doctors who tried camels went back to women".

Axel got a job in the neighboring town working at an "all-you-can-eat" restaurant. The place was filled with the obese and the elderly. It was a nightmare. The older patrons shuffled, leaned on each other and stood in one spot staring at food without getting any. Some of them talked to the food! All this got on Axel's nerves, so he installed a speaker under different food areas.

When someone began to talk to the roast or the potatoes Axel would answer them. If they stayed too long at the salad bar, Axel would say, "Lady how long can you look at lettuce? There isn't a lot of variety in lettuce." He was "let go" from this position, but he had found something he liked in speakers. They had potential!!

Next he installed a speaker under the hood of his car near the radiator. This was connected to a 'power" microphone inside the car. About sixty-five miles from Briar Patch was a huge metroplex, just the place to try his new trick. He drove downtown among fifty to sixty story buildings where the acoustics from his sound system would really vibrate. That part of town was full of homeless people, weirdo's, prostitutes, pimps and creeps. It was considered a "burned out" area in need of redevelopment. In short, it was tailor made for Axel.

He would wait at red lights for unusual people to cross the street. As soon as he saw a prospect he would began to criticize and make fun of them. They would stop in the street and look around, not being able to tell where this was coming from. At this point he would pour on the verbal abuse even harder. All the people in cars around him would be laughing too, as well as folks on the sidewalk. No one ever caught him at this and he had enough sense to know when to leave town.

Axel had a one-eyed cousin he hung out with. The cousin was nick named, Odin (the one eyed father of the Viking god's). Odin's parents were some of the religious fanatics who closed down the local entertainment that they saw as "evil".

This religious sect insisted on pissing to the east! This was extremely difficult if urinals were placed on walls facing west.

Axel and Odin would go the movies in a neighboring town and when Odin returned home his parents could smell the popcorn on him. "Boy", they would say, "Have you been to the house of the devil?" (This is what they called the movies). "Yes, I have," he said, "and it was good and I liked it." At this point they would beat Odin severely, but he always had his opinion and his say. He never backed down, never lied and always went back to the movies.

Knowing that Odin's eyesight was poor, Axel decided to pull a trick on him. One night the two of them went to see a wolf man movie. When Axel let Odin out at his home Axel began to get into his wolf man costume that he had prepared for this prank. He had purchased the fangs at the magic shop and the facial hair was taken from an old horse hair couch. Axel glued the hair right on his face.

Because these were the days of pre-air conditioning, Odin slept on a screened back porch in the summer. Axel crept up by the window where Odin's bed was. When he was near the bed, he looked Odin in the face and scratched on the screen with his claws going, "Wolf, Wolf"!

Odin shot out of bed, grabbed his shotgun and began blasting away in the yard. His parents woke up and confronted him saying, "Boy, what the hell are you doing?" "There's a monster out here?" "I'll monster your ass," said the Father. Axel could hear them thrashing Odin and him protesting that there really was a monster out there.

Since the first stunt went so well, Axel decided to try the same thing at his Aunt's house. She was watching her TV when Axel began scratching on her window screen and growling. Her eyesight must have been worse than Odin's because she mistook Axel for a common prowler. The lady phoned the Sheriff who just happened to be close by. Axel was running through bushes in the night with cops chasing him and sirens going off all around. Arriving at home, his problems were not over because the horsehair glued to his face was extremely difficult to remove. Odin still swears there was a monster out there and the Aunt still believes an ugly prowler scratched on her screen.

Chapter 9

B. O. Sharp was a gentle soul, despite his towering strength and menacing appearance. He had a lot of pets that frequented his shack. Because B. O. couldn't afford pets; he just made pets of whatever presented itself. He had a pet flying squirrel and a pet skunk. The skunk usually stayed at home, as she was a day sleeper. Rose Bud, the skunk, had dug a burrow under some old carpet in the back yard. When B. O. went to town he would pull back the carpet and see if Rose Bud was awake and wanted to go, too. In most cases she declined the invitation and let him know by reaching up and pulling the carpet back in place.

"Useless", the squirrel was also nocturnal, but would often allow himself to be persuaded for the promise of some town food. Useless rode and also slept in B. O.'s shirt pocket. Arriving at the diner, B. O. would order his meal. It wouldn't be long before the squirrel smelled the food and you would see two tiny hands grab the top of the pocket. Soon after that a small pixie face would pop up to look around. Useless wouldn't come out unless B. O. brought him out of the pocket. To this squirrel a pocket is security. This was especially true in day time hours. B. O. would hand Useless bits of food to eat and sometimes place him on the counter to get his own food from B. O's plate. On these occasions, Useless would grab crumbs and scurry back to the pocket to eat in some privacy. People who witnessed this were always captivated by it. To see that little tiny squirrel gently cared for by that great big man, seemed to captivate even the most cynical people.

Rose Bud went with B. O. at night and enjoyed eating bugs under town lights, which attracted many crickets and moths. B. O. kept Rose Bud on a harness with a leash when in town. As all skunks are born near sighted it was possible she could be run over by a car.

During the month of December skunks always seek other skunks, for romantic purposes. It wasn't too long until B. O. noticed a big male hanging around. Big AL, as B. O. called him, wasn't interested in becoming someone's pet. He was here to do business! B. O. left Big Al alone as he could tell that Al was carrying a big load of stink. Al would rock from side to side when he walked. He was actually sloshing with the weight of his liquid armament.

The next spring, Rose Bud had a litter of the cutest baby skunks. They are born hairless and with their eyes closed. Baby skunks look something like small mice. In a few weeks they open their eyes and began to "fur out."

In time B. O.'s place became (the skunk farm). It was also known as "Polecat Mountain." Having entirely too many skunks about the place, B. O. began to look for appropriate homes for them.

B. O. had not de-scented any of the skunks. If one does not make loud noises or threatening movements around them they remain calm. However, he failed to mention this to a lady who was interested in adoption. She was quite taken with the skunks, as they have unique mannerisms and personality. A raccoon, on the other hand, will tear up ones house and a opossum is a boring animal with absolutely no personality. Arriving home with her new skunk, the lady released it in the house.

Unfortunately, she also had a small yapping dog! These types of dogs are considered worthless by some like B. O. He commonly referred to them as, "turd hounds." This particular one was a Pomeranian. Skunk and Pomeranian quickly eyed each other! The dog rushed at the skunk, barking and raising all kinds of hell! The skunk bristled up and seemed to puff up to twice its normal size. Every hair stood erect and the tail looked exactly like a Christmas tree. As the dog closed in, the skunk twisted its body into a "U" or horseshoe shape. This is to see where to properly aim its shot. Skunks actually don't enjoy this and will refrain if at all possible. However, if sufficiently threatened or surprised they will discharge in a big way. The first white men who recorded encountering skunks in the new world were French trappers who dubbed it, "the stinking beast."

In this particular case nature took its course and the dog, the furniture, the carpet and the house were all generally and liberally anointed. The actual spray is a yellow amber liquid, which is sprayed a distance of ten feet before it begins to "mist." At this point the mist molecules stick to any surface. Tomato juice does not remove them, as it is mythically believed to do. The odor must simply wear off with time.

That very day the big Cadillac roared into B. O.'s yard. The door opened and the skunk flew out. The car left in a spray of gravel with the tires squealing when they hit paved road. B. O. reluctantly agreed to de-scent any future transactions.

In the summer Ruff Brier began to go to nearby corn fields. There she would disrobe entirely and sun bathe among the corn. One day Bookworm was riding his bicycle beside that particular corn patch. Suddenly, and without warning, Ruff emerged from the field still unclad and encountered the young man. Having never seen a naked hag before, Bookworm was shocked. "Boy," she shouted, "what day is it?" "It's Saturday," Worm replied. "How do you know that?" shouted Ruff. "I always get my hair cut on Saturday, so since I did that today, it must by Saturday." At this point, Ruff began to brandish her butcher knife and scream, "suck titty baby, suck titty baby." Bookworm's bad haircut (from Firewater Barstool) stood straight up and he preformed a "wheelie" on the bicycle getting out of there. This particular experience may have "scarred" him somewhat, as he was very late in developing an interest in women.

About this time some high school girls began to visit Ruff at lunch. They would return to school laughing about what Ruff had said as they related their experience to others. For some unknown reason, Ruff talked loudly and shouted often in her conversation. Maybe she thought that if she talked loudly, people would listen. Or, perhaps she thought it would lend validity to her comments.

On this particular day she was imparting her sagely wisdom to Bunny and to Crash. She said, "You girls stay away from these god-damn old men. All they want to do is fudge you!" "I've got a god-damn man who visits me from the railroad (actually, this was a rail traveling hobo). He sounds like a freight train when he's trying to get a little pussy! But he's a rich son-of-a-bitch. He's got a fifty dollar car and a two hundred dollar house!" Stories like this began to circulate all over the school. Everyone looked forward to what outrageous things Ruff would say next. Unfortunately, only the older girls had enough courage to approach Ruff in her lair. When teachers found out about this the activity was strongly discouraged.

It wasn't long after this that Ruff showed up at Dr. Feelgoods office. Like most business owners, Feelgood disliked dealing with Ruff. She ran paying customers off, but everyone accommodated her, as she was seen as the ward of the town. Ruff never paid for any service or commodity. It just never seemed to occur to her to be necessary. On this particular day Ruff said, "Dr., I've got some god-damn bugs in my bush." "What?" said Feelgood, "I don't understand what you mean?" "God-damn it, those sons-of-bitches crawl and bite me. Do you want to see?" She began to disrobe! "No," said Feelgood, "I think I understand now! Bugs in the bush, you say. Well, you don't need a prescription for that. Just go to the drug store and ask for some blue ointment. Spread this on yourself and that should solve your problem."

By the time Ruff got to the drug store she had forgotten the name of the medication. The storeowner waited on her immediately, to get her out of his place. She said, "Feelgood sent me here to get something but I forgot the god-damn name of that shit." "What's it for?" said the pharmacist. "It's to kill some of those bastard bugs in my bush." "Oh!" said the pharmacis thinking it is for outdoor plants, "you must want Parris Green." "That stuff did have a color to it. I guess that's the shit!" Parris Green is a very toxic poison and is not sold today.

Time passed and one day Dr. Feelgood saw Ruff going down the road. "Say, Ms. Briar, did you get rid of all the bugs in the bush?" "Hell yes," said Ruff. "That god-damn shit killed all those bug in my bush. It also killed the bush and hospitalized two bums off the railroad.

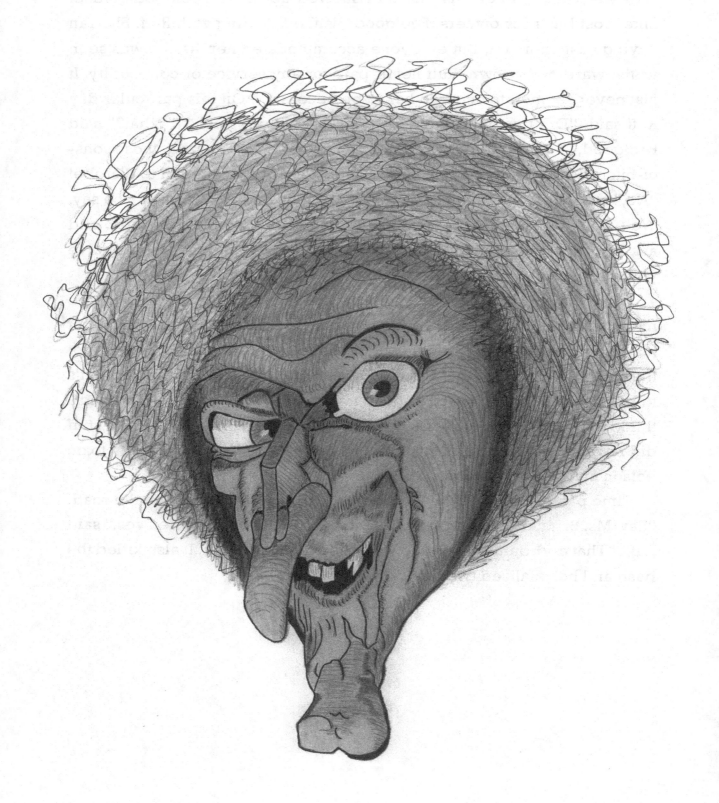

Chapter 10

Dr. Feelgood had a very plush office. It was large and spacious with marble statues and ornate mahogany paneling on the walls. In the back of his office was a small broom closet less than two feet wide, which was obviously for storage. It was molded right into the mahogany décor. This small space, approximately eighteen inches deep, had a false back installed in it. The false back lead into a hidden rest room facility. Both the outside door and the false back were fixed to snap back in place automatically when opened and released. This was for the doctor's use and everyone at the clinic was familiar with it.

One day Crash decided to apply for clerical work at Feelgood's office. Crash didn't know the Dr. very well, but assumed he would be someone satisfactory to work for. The office manager gave Crash some application forms to fill out. She was left alone and was busily working on them when the doctor burst into the room. Without saying a word he ran to his bathroom and disappeared. Obviously he had immediate need of the facility. However, to Crash, who didn't know there was another room behind the wall, this was extremely disturbing. Time passed and the doctor did not re-emerge from the broom closet. Eventually the office manager came into check on Crash's progress. Finding Crash in a very distraught condition, she asked, "What's the problem dear?" Crash replied, "Dr. Feelgood just ran in here and jumped into a drawer! And he's still in it." Poor Crash thought she was about to go to work for a lunatic. Nevertheless she accepted the job.

As time passed Crash became bored with clerical work. Her new passion was to become a police officer. By this time the doctor, who had no children of his own, had begun to act as a father figure for Crash. He knew Crash was not suited for police work and tried to persuade her not to attempt that move. He would say, "If you stop a three-time loser just out of the penitentiary, he has nothing to lose by killing you. Besides, men are often offended by female officers. What will you do if you confront a six foot six inch, two hundred and fifty pound habitual rapist?" Crash, who by now visualized herself as "Jane Wayne," responded, "I can handle it!" The frustrated doctor replied, "Well, if you can handle it, then why is there rape in the first place?" Naturally, Crash had no answer for that comment, but was still determined to be a police officer.

She eventually got a job at the sheriff's department. Crash liked to cruise the back roads, where she was less likely to have an accident, looking for crime to crush. That night Casanova and some friends were returning from a long trip. They were far from any town when Casanova announced a desperate need for a toilet facility. Being too far from any normal bathroom facility, he chose a secluded spot in the country for this emergency. On a backcountry road, far from any houses, they stopped. Casanova couldn't have gone another mile. By now it was pitch black and there was no one around for miles, they surmised! Casanova jumped the fence and ran out about twenty yards into a dark field.

About that time officer Crash appeared and suspected something illegal might be going on. She was especially suspicious about drugs and illegal contraband.

Casanova's friends explained that they were only out there because there was no rest room facility anywhere to be had. Not believing them, she decided to check it out. Crash had in her possession the most powerful spotlight made. It was a two million candle power that made night time as bright as day. Shined in an individuals face, it could damage their retina. Crash turned the spotlight into the field and flipped it on. Fortunately for Casanova, his back was to the spectators. Unfortunately for Crash, she saw Casanova drop a load without a commode. Crash didn't say another word. She turned off the spotlight and drove away. The next day she resigned from police work.

Since Dr. Feelgood's counseling was not effective on Crash, it took something like this event to get through to her. She reapplied and was welcomed back at her old clerical job.

One day it snowed, so Crash walked to work. Driving was always hazardous for Crash, but driving in snow would be especially risky. When she approached the clinic she saw smoke pouring out of the doctor's car trunk. Believing that the car was on fire, Crash ran to the rear of the car and, finding it unlocked, jerked open the trunk.

There she discovered Dr. Feelgood rolled up in a fetal position smoking a cigar. Suddenly Crash got a flashback of her first day at Feelgood's office.

On that particular day she saw Feelgood jump into a drawer. Now he's rolled up in a wad smoking a cigar in the trunk of a car.

As the Dr. was caught at this strange behavior he began to crawl out of the trunk and offer some explanation. The very embarrassed Dr. explained that his wife had forbidden him to smoke anymore. She gave him absolutely no time to taper off smoking. She just demanded he stop now, cold turkey! Being too "whipped" to stand up to the witch, he was desperate to find a smoking place that she couldn't smell or catch him in the act. This eliminated the house, the job, the garage, etc. It was too cold to smoke outside so he had deteriorated to becoming a "trunk smoker." It was the only place he could think of that he would be safe from her wrath.

Axel Fender had a flat bed hay truck that he used in the summer to haul loads of hay. This was dirty, hard work performed by people who were really in good shape, or were desperate for money. High school football players did it during the summer to stay in shape. Work was often eighteen-hour days and usually six days a week. On your time off one would eat and sleep. That was all the time one had. This process continued all three months of the summer unless it rained. People who aspired to build themselves up physically were drawn to it. These were pre-air conditioning days.

Since Bookworm was tired of living the life of a weakling, he hoped Axel would let him work on the hay truck. Axel had his doubts that Bookworm could stand up to that kind of abusive labor, but decided to give him a chance.

Hauling hay required at least three people, one to drive the truck, one to throw hay on the truck, and one to stack the hay. Axel drove, because he owned the truck. Besides, driving the hay truck didn't build you up, and didn't pay much either. Unless you happened to own the truck, which in this case, Axel did!

The next hardest job was stacking the hay. This took some skill because the loaded hay had to be driven to a location for unloading without falling off the truck. Axel gave Bookworm this job and demonstrated how to stack hay properly. The last and hardest job was pitching the hay bales on the truck. The one doing this job had to be able to throw bales increasingly higher as the load grew. Additionally this person had to walk from bale to bale throughout the entire field.

Animal X and B. O. Sharp were the premier hay haulers in the area and never hauled less than a thousand bales a day. At this time many applicants were available for this type of work. If you didn't have a summer job and you were high school age, you were somewhat disgraced. The pay was two cents a bale, which amounts to twenty dollars a day for one thousand bales in an eighteen hour day. In the nineteen-sixties people were glad to get such work. Today, no one will do it for any price. It was truly a different world.

Because most of the best workers were already working for other crews, Axel had to hire Catshit Looney. Catshit couldn't work for anyone who was weaker than he was, and if you couldn't out fight Catshit this could be problematic. Since Axel was stronger than Catshit and could definitely out fight him, the deal was struck. The other problem was Catshit having to work around Bookworm! This was like a dog working around a cat! It would be a problem for Catshit to refrain from doing bodily harm to Bookworm if he got the chance. Axel had to keep a constant eye on Catshit because of this.

An insurance company could have done well selling liability insurance against collateral damage from working with Catshit.

Bookworm showed up for work without any gloves. There were abandoned, worn out gloves in the truck cab, so Axel gave Bookworm two of these remnants. "But Axel," complained Bookworm, "these gloves are both for the same hand!" "Just turn one upside down," replied Axel. He could see that it was going to be a very long day.

Everything seemed to be going well until the first load was being hauled to the storage barn. Bookworm and Catshit were riding on top of the load and were passing through the town of Briar Patch. With nothing to do, Catshit began to try to pull off parts of Bookworm's anatomy. It was things Bookworm needed, like his arms for example. Axel was driving and couldn't hear Bookworm yelling for help. Fortunately for Bookworm, Briar patch had one signal light in the center of town suspended between telephone poles. This particular signal light was completely unlike any other. Most "stop and go" lights have red at the top, with amber in the center and green at the bottom. In Briar Patch this was just the opposite. Red and green were reversed. Perhaps it was simply installed upside down. The situation did not create a problem unless you were color blind. If a color blind person thought red and green were in the traditional places they could easily have a problem at this location. That signal light saved Bookworm on this particular day.

Catshit had all his attention focused on twisting the boys arm out of socket. He wasn't paying attention when the hay truck went under the light at approximately fifty miles per hour. The light caught Catshit in the head and knocked him off the load of hay and on to the pavement. Bookworm finally got Axel's attention and alerted him to the situation. They returned to the site of the incident and retrieved Catshit quickly. The fool was miraculously uninjured.

For all of Catshit's faults, he was tremendously resilient. Axel solved the situation by having Bookworm ride in the cab with him. He placed Catshit on the front fender, sitting with a headlight between his legs. This way Axel could keep an eye on both of them at the same time. The hay truck Axel owned did not have the hood on it at the time they were using it. It wasn't long until Catshit began to reach inside the engine and twist the distributor cap. The bastard was like an ape, he just couldn't leave things alone. His "tinkering" caused the engine to slow down and speed up accordingly, because this is where the spark plug wires all connect. Axel began to shout at him, "Catshit, you son-of-a-bitch, quit fucking with that distributor cap." Axel was simply ignored by Catshit, and the obnoxious behavior continued.

Quite suddenly, something rather bazaar happened! Because Catshit was sitting on a metal fender, and because there was an electrical short in the distributor cap, a tremendous jolt of electricity was discharged. A stream of blue fire passed through Catshit and shot him off the fender and into the ditch while the truck was traveling at approximately forty-five miles per hour.

Like any animal, Catshit was not fond of shock treatment. It was one of the few things he feared and respected. He seemed to settle down some so Axel thought the worst was behind them. However, it was not to be! While unloading the hay, Bookworm worked the upper level with Axel throwing hay into the loft and Catshit shuttled the bales between the two.

About half way through the load Axel heard Bookworm yelling for help. He found Catshit busily engaged in trying to get Bookworm's pants off of him. Axel had lost all patience with Catshit at this point and began to thrash him. He had to be careful not to get carried away to the point that Catshit was unable to work and yet still make his point.

An interesting thing about Axel was that while thrashing someone, he also talked to them at the same time. This was particularly humiliating because it demonstrated how easily he could control you. Sometimes he would "semi-sing" to people while he was working-them-over! Things like, "Santa bitch is a-coming to town," or perhaps this one, "I love New York in spring, how about you?" Axel would punch the person at the same _word_ in the song every time. So you knew when he was going to unload. He was so quick that it didn't matter. In the Santa bitch song he would always strike when he got to the word "town." In the New York song he would hit on the word "you." This sight never failed to either amuse or amaze spectators who witnessed it.

Finally, the trio stopped by the farm supply store and Axel purchased a cattle prod. It was a very powerful type that shot electricity several inches. This tended to keep Catshit in line for the duration of the job.

After the job was finished Catshit found an old compressor gage. He bolted this gage on to his bicycle handle bars, as this was his only transportation. He explained to people that this gage was his lightning detector. If he and the bicycle were ever struck by lightning, the gage would jump to "charge." At that point he would know to go faster. No one pointed out to him that the gage wasn't designed for that, or if in fact he was struck by lightning he would look like a burnt match and have no need of a gage to tell him anything!

Chapter 11

The Neanderthal-like family known to the locals as Creatures had robust bodies. They probably needed them to survive in their lifestyle. They had thick bones attached to massive, cable like, tendons needed to do daily work of chewing tough roots, lifting large logs, and digging food out of burrows. When stalking large animals, such as deer or wild hogs, the Creatures would kill the animals with their fists, hands, or clubs. If they had no weapons, they simply twisted their necks, sometimes to the point of decapitation. It is no wonder they were called "The Creatures" and likened to cave people.

Adult male Creatures did not discipline small Creature children, as adult males were considered too strong and might seriously injure one by accident. Discipline, therefore, fell to the female Creatures, who laid it on with a vengeance when it was needed.

Most Creatures disdained shoes. The bottoms of their feet were so thickly calloused they could walk through hot coals. Eventually, as years passed, their feet began to acquire the thickness of horses hooves on the bottom. Cold weather was ignored, as the feet were equally immune to cold as to heat. A few of the Creatures began to have foot problems in mid-October. If their skin texture was not the right oiliness, or had the wrong pH balance, deep cracks would develop where the calluses met ordinary skin. This condition was painful enough to cause the subject to wrap his feet in sacks during the winter. The sacks were held in place with twine. This seemed to alleviate the problem satisfactorily.

During hot summer days, the temperature could easily exceed one hundred degrees Fahrenheit. Creatures would walk to town on the hot asphalt roads. Upon arriving at the town's gas station, they would borrow a knife from the tire department. They would then slice the hot tar and gravel off the bottom of their feet like shucking oysters. All this was accomplished completely pain free.

If someone gave the Creatures a bag of flour they would promptly turn it into a wad of dough. When it was sufficiently textured a stick was run through the mass and held over an open fire. By slowly turning the stick they made their version of bread. As the clan had no way to store food, they ate all they could and threw the rest away. Wolf would always attempt to hide food by burying it – but this practice was strongly discouraged by Fox, who was always attempting to civilize the family.

Fox was probably the brightest family member. He was reminiscent of "Pinocchio" who was trying to be a "real" boy instead of a puppet. He could even be described as "Mr. Data" on Star Trek, who was ever attempting to become more human than android.

If the clan was out hunting and camped in a new place they had a ritual they followed at night. Before sleeping everyone would urinate into the campfire at the same time. This was the last act before retiring. It was not to extinguish the fire. The purpose was to determine what the hunting would be like the following day. The odor of scorched urine would spread out along the ground. It was believed that if a bobcat smells scorched urine he will involuntarily let out a loud screech! If a bobcat was near, the hunting would probably be poor, as the Creatures and bobcats often competed for similar food. One of the Creatures, named Bobcat, always screeched at the strong ammonia smell of burning urine. This supposedly is why he was named after the animal.

During Christmas season a well-meaning family brought a dozen hats out to the Creature family for gifts. The hats were arranged in sizes from the largest to the smallest. The largest was well in excess of size eight. The smallest was a bonnet for the smallest infant. The following day the senior head of the crew was seen in town wearing all of the hats at once. He had the largest hat on the bottom and smaller ones stacked on top of it, with the baby bonnet perched at the very tip. Needless to say, this display did not create a new trend in haberdashery (the wearing of hats).

All the Creatures seemed fascinated with gumball machines. Especially the type that ran around a maze before popping out the bottom. When they found any lost coins this is where they headed. Wolf always ate the gum after chewing it. Fox would reprimand him for this behavior. Fox would say, "The gum is only for chewing".

Wolf would answer, "If Wolf is going to the trouble to chew a thing he is also going to eat it too!" Wolf usually referred to himself in second or third person. I, or me was not part of his vocabulary.

One day Wolf found a quarter and put it into what he thought was a gum ball machine in the gas station restroom. He told Fox about it later. He said, "Wolf won't use the gum machine at the gas station anymore. It tastes just like rubber!"

Rats were a great delicacy for the Creatures. They never passed up a chance for a good rat roast. The local feed store and grain mill always had a rat problem. The Creatures were born rat catchers, so a deal was made between them to "de-rat" the places regularly. No one knows exactly what method the Creatures used to capture the rats. It was enough that it worked and people were content to leave it at that!

If the Creatures were especially hungry and in a hurry to eat they would just throw the dead rats on a pile of straw and set the whole thing on fire. No one bothered to skin or gut them beforehand. It is interesting to note that there is an identical practice in Taiwan. In that country it is an annual and celebrated event.

If the hunting of rats was particularly good the Creatures would roast the rats on sticks over the fire, much as we do hotdogs and marshmallows. They creatively called this method "Rat-on-a-stick." When Creatures were not hungry and not in any particular hurry to eat the rat bounty they might do something fancy, like creating a cuisine. The most creative rat dish was their famous "rat pie". This particular delicacy was served at Thanksgiving and other festive occasions, not that the Creatures followed any calendar or clock. If someone told them it was Thanksgiving or some holiday, they would attempt to act accordingly. The only time table they seemed to observe was the seasons. A thing got done in its own time and there was no stress.

Only the most daring adventurous people ever ate a holiday meal with the Creatures as a guest. The Creatures tried their best to be hospitable, but guests would feel obliged to "nibble" at things and suggest that they had already eaten earlier.

Wolf and Fox were cleaning out the rats at the local feed store one day. They carried the captured rats in what we call burlap bags, gunnysacks, or croker sacks. All of these are good rat transporters. Simply thrown over the shoulder, both men were carrying out their squealing, jumping bags of rats. Fox was always trying to be cordial to people. He paused on his way out of the store to ask some ladies if they would like to see some of the nice rats he and Wolf had caught. Both women squealed and quickly declined. Fox responded with, "Ahh, but they make such a delicious pie!"

It was about this time that the town of Briar Patch got a real sewage system. All of the old out-houses would now be obsolete. There were a few exceptions to this rule. Ruff Briar was not a tax-paying citizen, so she was by-passed in the sewage process. The County tax assessor dropped by her shack one day to see what might be taxable. Not knowing who he was dealing with, he ask, "Madam, how far does your property extend?" Ruff said, "Just out there to that goddamn shit house!" Ruff was not taxed.

Axel Fender had learned how to make small dynamite charges from his associate, Bookworm. He used these small explosives to blow up outhouses. Axel loved to see the shingles, lumber, and shit fly when he touched one of these off. Only Ruff's outhouse was exempt, as he knew she still used it. He did, however, lob a cherry bomb under it one day while she was occupying it. The bomb didn't damage the out-house. It did however, blow shit all over Ruff. She kicked the door off the out-house and ran about, brandishing her ever-present butcher knife and cussing loudly.

Boscoe Bad-ass was in town visiting relatives. His relatives were all there that day and the place was crowded. Simultaneously, several got the urge to try out the new facility and Boscoe was tired of waiting in line. He knew they had an old out-house out back and wasn't too proud to use it. He slipped out to the shack with his newspaper in hand. Axel never suspected that someone might actually still use one of these, when there was now indoor plumbing. It was with great surprise after he blew this one up, that he discovered a person occupying it at the time.

Boscoe sat among the ruins of what was the out-house. He was spattered with shit, his clothes, hair, and beard were scorched off of him and the newspaper he had been reading was only two scraps of paper, one in each hand! Not realizing what had truly happened, Boscoe said, "Damn, I'm glad I didn't let that one go in the kitchen."

Billy Bob McKnob was arrested in a near-by town. It seems that he decided to urinate in public at the town square. This was extremely noticeable behavior outside of Briar Patch. McKnob got himself a court-appointed lawyer who claimed that this should be dismissed because it was simply "an act of nature." McKnob didn't help his case any by shouting in court, "I'm guilty, I did it, lock me up." The judge decided to make McKnob do community service. They put him to work in a convenience store.

McKnob would say dirty things to customers that sounded like things people in business always say. The customers are so accustomed to it that they don't really pay attention to what you say, and they would pass it off, not really realizing what was actually said.

For example, McKnob would tell people that were leaving the store – "Fuck you now, and come back!" – or – "I beg your hard-on!" – or – "Please keep a civil tongue in my ass!" Sometimes he would say, "Did you fuck a goat?" When someone would say "what?" he would respond with, "Did you forget your coat?" No one ever caught on, or believed they were hearing incorrectly.

McKnob was cleaning his pistol one day while sitting in front of the gas station. During this process he accidentally shot himself in the foot. He then began to hop around on one foot while holding the injured one in both hands and cussing loudly.

The Creature clan was passing by the gas station and did not see McKnob shoot himself. They felt that they were missing out on something however, and all of them began to grab one foot, hop about and cuss loudly. Soon McKnob and approximately a dozen Creatures were hopping and cussing.

This unlikely scene caused traffic to halt, as drivers speculated on what this strange ritual was all about.

**Damn! I'm glad I didn't let
that one go in the kitchen!**

Chapter 12

While still in high school, Bunny and Crash began to search for jobs. Farm labor was about all that was available in and around Briar Patch. They both got jobs hoeing gardens. This work didn't last long, as there weren't many garden owners that needed any help. When all the work was exhausted Bunny and Crash traveled to a larger town to the Department of Unemployment.

They had to stand in line until their turn came at the desk. When they finally got to speak to someone, they were asked, "What type of employment were you last engaged in?" Crash loudly announced, "We're hoers". All work stopped and it got so quiet that you could hear an angel fart. After some explanation, the interview continued.

With their lack of education and work skills, manual labor was all the work available. The interviewer explained that this type of work was available only to men. Crash became indignant and said, "I can do anything a damn man can do!" There was an old man in line behind them. He asked, "Can you scratch your scrotum?" Bunny inquired, "What's a scrotum?" Crash and Bunny were told to come back after they finished high school and when they were at least eighteen years old.

A few years later after Bunny was married and Animal-X was in Viet Nam, she decided to go to college.

During a human anatomy class the professor said, "The male penis is a muscle. Bunny raised her hand and remarked, "I thought it was a bone." Annoyed at being interrupted, the professor replied, "It probably was when <u>you</u> saw it!"

As Bunny's behavior worsened, she openly propositioned people. One day at the local diner she approached B.O. Sharp. "B.O.," she asked, "Can you help me? I've got an itchy pussy!"

Far from the most intelligent citizen, B.O. said, "I'm sorry Ms. Bunny; I don't know nothin' 'bout them foreign cars."

Crash continued to work for Dr. Feelgood. One day the doctor's "bitch of a wife" came by the clinic and while she was there she invited Crash to one of her social gatherings. Crash was thrilled and readily accepted the invitation. On the day of the party Crash arrived on time, but didn't see anyone else there yet. Coming up the sidewalk, she saw the doctor's wife lean out the window of her house and ask Crash to go around back. Thinking the front door was damaged in some way, Crash made her way to the back door. Once she was inside the kitchen the doctor's wife strapped an apron on Crash and instructed her how to serve the real guests. Crash was mortified though she did not complain to the doctor as she felt her job at the office could be in danger.

Several people moved into the Briar Patch boarding house a few years after their graduation from high school. B.O. Sharp moved there when his shack burned down and Animal-X moved in when his marriage with Bunny failed. Bookworm and Axel Fender eventually found residence there as well.

Rent was only eight dollars a week. This seemed reasonable until you saw the full extent of the accommodations. Many times the headboard of the bed was half eaten away by termites and the bathroom was a large community affair, located at the end of the hall. This bathroom had many sinks, showers, and toilets, all arranged in rows. The ground floor had a long board that had fallen off the bottom of the building and ran full length of the showers. It was not uncommon to see possums and other small wildlife coming in for a drink of water while someone was showering.

Casanova lived on the second floor of the boarding house. He was often too drunk to negotiate his way to the toilet. To remedy this problem Casanova simply urinated out his window. This behavior eventually caused his screen to rust out which allowed all sorts of insects access to his dwelling. From outside, you could spot Casanova's window easily. It was the one with the long yellow stripe reaching to the ground. With the boarding house painted white, yellow really stood out noticeably.

Casanova liked to raid the boarding house kitchen late at night after a drinking binge. One night he came in drunk and found a pot of what he thought was stew on the stove. Casanova wolfed it down and went to bed. The next day someone was loudly complaining about the loss of their dog food. Apparently the refrigerator had been cleaned out and all the leftovers

I'm sorry Miss Bunny. I don't know
<u>nothin</u> bout them foreign cars.

for approximately three months of age or older were sitting out for disposal. Casanova had a very bad taste in his mouth that day and, to this day, will not eat stew.

All the tenants knew each other and everyone got along well. Axel and Animal-X began to play tricks on each other while they lived there. This all started when Axel urinated in Animal's after-shave lotion, causing Animal's face to break-out badly. Animal retaliated by dumping ten large bags of cow manure in Axel's room. A few days later Axel caught a ten-pound carp while fishing. He got under Animal's car and put the carp on top of the car's oil pan. Two days later Animal had a date with a new female acquaintance. It was very hot that August evening and the carp began to stink badly. Both Animal and the woman began to look at each other strangely. Each of them believed they were smelling the other person. Animal found the dead fish the next day, however the woman wouldn't go out with him again.

Axel would wait until Animal was sleeping at night. He would then pick his door lock, sneak into the room, plug in his electric blanket and turn up the dial to "maximum heat." Re-locking the door, he would stand outside for awhile until he heard Animal spring out of bed like a scorched cat, cussing a blue streak.

Animal seized Axel's pillow, tore it open, and dumped hog manure in it. He then sewed it up and left it where he had found it. Every night when Axel went to bed, he smelled pig shit! Although he tore his room apart looking for it, he never discovered where it was and slept on it for months.

Axel poured half a bottle of Nair Hair Remover into Animal's shampoo. A few days later clumps of hair began to fall out of Animal's head. The hair on his body behaved in a similar fashion. Animal suspected it was the vitamins that he was taking. He said "I knew there might be side effects to vitamins this strong, but this is too much!" His next purchase at the feed store was medicine for mange.

The things they did to each other got progressively worse. One night while Animal was out late on a date, Axel dismantled Animal's bed and re-assembled it in the middle of the parking lot. When Animal arrived at the boarding house it was very late and although he recognized the situation, he was too tired to deal with it. Animal simply said, "To hell with it!" and went to bed in the parking lot.

All would have gone well except for a drunk driver. Around two a.m. the drunk came roaring into the parking lot and barely stopped short of plowing into the bed. The sleeping man came awake with the headlights on bright and the car bounding up and down only a few inches from his feet. A loud altercation developed. The boarding house owner, (better known as "Broom Hilda") who was meaner than a dog shitting tacks, swept down upon the two with righteous indignation. Both were severely chastised and Animal had to dismantle the bed and re-assemble it in his room. After this incident Axel and Animal both agreed to a truce, as neither one wanted to be evicted.

Bandit Hanging would never challenge B.O. Sharp but it didn't stop him from "messing" with B.O.'s simple mind. Once, Bandit convinced B.O. that he might have worms. The very idea of worms crawling around inside his body terrified poor B.O. He became obsessed with the idea. The next time B.O. has a bowel movement he began to examine the feces looking for worms. He had been told this was the way to know for sure. He didn't understand that this parasite is too small to ordinarily be seen without a microscope.

B.O. was down on his knees with kitchen fork in hand busily going through the process of searching in the commode. At that precise moment Bookworm entered the community bathroom and saw B.O. To Bookworm it looked like B.O. Sharp was eating rather than searching. Bookwork was shocked and appalled. He reported what he had seen to Axel Fender but this was dismissed by Axel as a joke.

Not finding any worms, B.O. phoned a clinic in a near-by town as to what procedure was necessary to determine if someone had worms. He was informed by the clinic that to determine if worms were present, they would need a "warm stool". Not being able to produce a warm stool on command, B.O. decided to save his next one in a cracker box. Said box was placed in the oven and the temperature was turned to "warm". When he would get off work, he would rush the "warm stool" to the clinic. This was his plan.

While B.O. was at work Bookworm smelled something awful coming from B.O.'s room. Upon investigating he found the cracker box in the oven, turd and all. "My God," said Bookworm, "now he's cooking the shit!"

97

No one believed Bookworm but he continued to watch B.O. carefully. As soon as B.O. got off work he grabbed the warm stool in the cracker box and headed for the clinic. Consequently, Bookworm assumed that B.O. was doing "take-out" meals. At the clinic it was explained to B.O. that a warm stool means a fresh stool. Not one that has been in an oven all day. To make a long story short, B.O. discovered he did not have worms and Bookworm was able to put his fears aside that B.O. might have lost his wits.

These and other situations were continually being instigated by Bandit Hanging. If Bandit had any social graces at all, his garage would have been the perfect focal point for aspiring young mechanics. Instead, the man was vile, sour, and disagreeable. He grudgingly tolerated people if they knew approximately which particular part of their car was malfunctioning. If you knew you were having a transmission or a clutch problem he might be civil to you.

When Bookworm got his first car he was very proud and went to Bandit's garage for a tune-up on the vehicle. Bandit always verbally abused young boys. Poor Bookworm was no exception. Bandit said, "Bookworm, you're not worth a shit for nothing, are you? You probably can't even turn a wrench. The only thing you're good for is to read books. You're never going to amount to anything when you grow-up! I heard you've even got a little dick."

Bookworm didn't have a strong self-image and this bashing from an adult didn't help it at all.

However, sometimes you can push even someone like Bookworm too far. Bookworm would probably have let the matter go, except that Bandit had insulted his "weenie".

Bookworm made a special trip to a porn shop in the metroplex where he purchased the largest rubber dildo available. This particular one was at least two feet long, flexible, and colored bright green. The plan was to wear the thing sticking out the front of his pants and jump in front of Bandit when he exited his office.

Bookworm wore a long trench coat that day, to conceal the "appendage." He arrived at the garage and waited. Someone he thought was Bandit was coming through the office door. Bookworm threw back his trench coat, took the dildo in both hands, and brandished it about, yelling, "Stick this up your ass!" Unfortunately the person coming out of Bandit's office wasn't Bandit at all. It was a woman from another town that promptly screamed and fainted. Bookworm ran before he could be identified. All that saved Bookworm was that the woman couldn't identify him. She phoned the sheriff's department and got the desk sergeant.

Since the call was coming from Briar Patch the sergeant no doubt figured it was some lunatic. The woman said, "Officer, a little man jumped out at me awhile ago. He had a big green dick and he took that thing in both hands and snapped it at me." Thinking that surely this was a joke, the desk sergeant began to laugh until tears rolled down his face and he said, "Maybe we should charge him with assault with a deadly weapon!" The woman was not amused and promptly went "over his head". The sergeant was then reprimanded by the captain.

The incident of the little man with the large green dick got all over town. Somehow the little man also became green in the story's retelling. Firewater Barstool loudly proclaimed that the person in question was a frequent visitor to his barbershop. However, Firewater had also witnessed unicorns, mermaids, and leprechauns in his shop when he drank his hair tonic.

There were even rumors that the little green man was from Mars. Bookworm buried the dildo under the floor of the family barn and hoped all the excitement would just "go away".

Bandit also sold reconstructed lawnmowers. Old Lady McSwindle (Jimmy the Louse's maternal grandmother) decided to "con" Bandit into selling her one at a reduced price.

One of the McSwindle's favorite tricks was to sound religious in her business transactions. "Mr. Hanging, me and Jesus want to buy that lawn mover, but me and Jesus only got forty dollars". Bandit replied, "I can't speak for Jesus but you better get your ass a job, cause you're looking at a 150 dollar mower."

Chapter 13

Small carnivals occasionally toured the lesser-populated towns collecting money for charity. These gypsy-type shows were not taken seriously because they usually involved many of the local citizens as exhibits. The mayor, for example, would be the wild man from Borneo. The high school principal would most likely be seated at the baseball throw water dunk.

People paid a mere five or ten cents at each exhibit and it was fun to see people you know doing silly things. Town folks also operated the rides and were in charge of most of the exhibits too.

Bandit Hanging's wife suggested that Bandit should be the wild man from Borneo. It would be a status thing for her. Bandit didn't really want anything to do with any of this, but knew he would "catch hell" if he refused.

The wild man suit looked something like "the Flintstones" might wear. It was a one-strap leopard suit complete with a wooden club. The "wild man" was supposed to jump at people, growl, and swing his club around. Bandit entered the cage in his full cave man regalia.

Shortly after Bandit got inside the cage he discovered he had a very urgent need. Mother nature called mightily and it was not just a gas attack. He approached the cage door and asked to be let out for this emergency. It was his bad luck that Bookworm was in charge of the door lock. Bookworm still remembered all the verbal abuse Bandit heaped upon him at the garage, so he ignored Bandit's request.

At this point Bandit began to get angry and threaten Bookworm. He pointed out quite specifically that this was a serious matter and not a joke.

The Worm looked him straight in the eye and said, "The more you shit, the wilder you'll get!" Bandit began to yell for help and a crowd gathered, believing this was all a part of his act. As he became more desperate Bandit began to use his club wildly on the cage door. He screamed obscenities at Bookworm and dashed about the cage, pulling at the bars and trying his best to escape. All this only served to further delight the crowd, which grew increasingly bigger by the moment. Everyone was laughing at this unexpected show of public spirit and hidden talent. Bandit became red-faced and began to howl. The local paper was taking pictures when Bandit released a shit storm toward the camera. People scattered in all directions and it was speculated that Bandit had taken the role of "wild man" to a new level. His wife was not pleased with his performance. The next day the local paper headlines read "Shit Storm In Texas."

This particular carnival had a trained bear. The bear was a regular black one rather than a grizzly. The black bear usually average about six hundred pounds, while the world record grizzly is about four times heavier.

The bear in question was trained to wrestle people. His claws were trimmed and he wore a muzzle, so he would not seriously hurt anyone. However, this bear knew a few tricks. He would pull a person into a "bear hug" and scrape his muzzle all over the face and head of his foe. This would cause skin abrasions and loss of hair. If someone managed a headlock on the bear, the bear would simply curl into a ball and try to kick your face off.

Casanova's family would all get roaring drunk and try their luck with the bear. They discovered that being drunk did not impress the bear, or make one a better opponent. It does, however, lessen the pain, which the bear will inflict upon your person during the melee.

The local preacher was running the bear exhibit when Casanova took his turn at the bear. Each contestant was allotted ten minutes to "impress" the bear. Casanova was ready to get out long before his allotted ten minutes was up. He shouted, "Preacher, let me out of here!"

The reverend replied. "Have faith son, the Lord of host is with thee." Casanova then said, "You know I love the Lord, but in this cage the bear is the host and a piss poor one at that!!

Meanwhile, something really interesting occurred during the ongoing bear fights. One of the Creature family was persuaded to fight the bear!

Before we get to that famous contest we should describe the Creatures in even greater depth.

No one was sure what the Creatures were capable of. They were retiring and non-violent. Everyone knew they were strong but no conflicts had ever existed to test them. The Creatures possessed no self-esteem, so they were never offended. They never stole anything and were not interested in the

102

town's women. Therefore they were never at odds with other people. Their formidable physical appearance and the fact that they usually traveled in groups kept the curious from testing them.

There were other Creature clans besides the one outside Briar Patch. Each clan foraged about, in roughly a twenty-five mile radius. Creature females never came to town. They stayed close to the temporary camp, picked berries, nuts, and dug roots. Their area of hunting was about one-fourth that of a mountain lion. If an area became depleted or hunted out, they moved on to another area or abandoned farmhouse.

Each family group functioned almost like a wolf pack. There was one alpha male and one alpha female. This was the breeding pair for the area. Other members of the pack were older brothers and sisters who helped rear the younger members. The pack could also contain aunts, uncles, and sometimes cousins. None of these were breeders and this kept their numbers low enough to sustain the availability of food supply.

If a new pack was needed, there would be a meeting of clans to determine which pair would become the alpha's for the new group. This prevented inbreeding and kept their numbers in check. The Creatures seemed to know where other clans were located. They were fairly secretive about when and where they gathered and no outsiders were ever in attendance.

The most formidable looking Creature in the Briar Patch clan was an imposing individual named "Man Eater". No one ever asked where he got his name. Man Eater was unusual even among his own strange people. He possessed unusually large and long hands. His hands could span the steering wheel of a car, with his fingers touching the entire outside circle. The most amazing thing about Man Eater was how he reacted to wasp nests. He hated wasps and never passed up a chance to kill them. If he saw a nest of wasps he would approach them and suddenly grab the entire nest with one hand. He was so quick that no wasps ever escaped. At this point he would squeeze the nest that he had pulled from its location. In a few seconds he would open his hand and drop the contents. All the wasps would be dead and the nest crushed. It was never known if he was stung during this activity. If he was, he never showed any visible signs of it. People marveled at the sight, but it was never duplicated, or even attempted, by anyone else.

It was Man Eater who got in the bear cage that day. He had watched the other people wrestle the bear and knew what to expect from the bear. Also, Man Eater was not a drinker because no one ever gave the Creature family alcohol. There is no way to predict what might have happened if they did.

As the bear approached Man Eater, he grabbed the bear with both of his monstrous hands. Each hand had control of both the bear's paws. The bear was unable to drag Man Eater into his usual "bear hug". The bear also discovered that he couldn't extract himself from Man Eater's grip. Those unusual hands wrapped completely around the bear's arms and at that point the animal realized something was wrong. Man Eater began to knee and kick the bear on the body and on both its feet. The bear broke away and Man Eater chased it around the cage. The owner of the bear stopped the contest and asked Man Eater to come out, in the belief he was abusing the bear. If there was ever a question in anyone's mind about confronting the Creatures, this display laid it to rest.

The Creature clan gene pool must have been something rare. Extremes ranged from wilderness living primitives to the pre-human look. Many felt that the Creature clan's human DNA could have traces of Neanderthal and Sasquatch hanging from the family tree. However, the Creature DNA was never too closely examined because it could be discerning to discover that there might even be monkeys somewhere in one's family.

It must have been poetic justice in the incident of Bookworm humiliating Bandit Hanging. Because soon after the public beshating display hosted by Bookworm there was a similar incident. This time Bookworm was the star of the show. It seems that a new fast food service was testing its wares in Briar Patch. There was nothing like it for miles around and Bookworm was fortunate enough to get a job at the grand opening.

He wasn't feeling well that day and had stopped by his grandmother's house on the way to work. He mentioned to her that his stomach was acting up, which turned out to be a fatal mistake around Ms. Neill. Her generation often believed the universal cure for all maladies was a strong laxative. They gave out laxatives for everything from hangnails to VD. So, naturally a laxative was forced on Bookworm before he could leave.

Arriving at work was a madhouse. Everyone in town wanted to try out the new place and traffic was backed up for blocks. Bookworm was put to work grilling food in the kitchen next to the drive-through window. He soon discovered that his troubled digestive tract boosted by his grandma's strong laxative was about to go off like the volcano, Krakatoa.

Bookworm alerted his manager to the situation but was ignored because the busy manager was new in his job. He didn't want to get behind, thus looking bad on opening day. A heated argument between the two went on for some time. The manager said he would fire Bookworm if he left his station during this rush. Finally, after holding back nature for approximately an hour Bookworm lost it completely, right at the grill. He went to the restroom shaking crap out of both pant legs along the way. That was the end of his job! He was relating the incident to his mother and she asked, "Why didn't you just go?" He said, "I did!"

Coming home from school one day Bookworm saw a large crowd gathered near his house. A neighbor woman was yelling and screaming causing more people to assemble. Pushing through the crowd Bookworm discovered his hound dog (named R. J.) having sex with the neighbor's fluffy, fuzzy housedog. The woman would screech and holler, "My baby is being raped!" Aroused by the commotion, Bookworm's dad came out of the house, saw the situation, and knew the solution right away.

"Boy," he said to Bookworm, "go get a bucket of cold water and throw it on that bitch." (This will usually cause dogs to "disengage".)

Bookwork ran into the house, filled a bucket of cold water, and returned to the scene of the crime. He immediately drenched the squalling woman from top to bottom. The entire crown was laughing at the woman as she angrily stormed back to her house. Bookworm's father did not punish the boy, as he figured it was a natural and reasonable mistake, considering the woman's behavior. Bookworm's father further instructed him that a person could always tell what time of day it was by watching a bitch in heat. For example, if one sees six dogs running down the street – it's five after one. If one sees eleven dogs running down the street, it's ten after one. (Very valuable information)

Chapter 14

The Goodbody family routinely gave switchblades, brass knuckles, and police slap sticks to each other for Christmas. Casanova had a simple formula for his successes (a formula which he sometimes forgot). His best fighting was done when he was drunk and his best "wrenching" was done when he was sober.

Casanova was drunk one night at a nightclub. The evening steadily deteriorated as he continued to drink.

One of the women strippers came over to Casanova's table and said, "I'll dance on your table for twenty dollars." Casanova responded, "I'm not rich! Could you just shit in the ashtray for ten dollars?" The stripper replied, "They pay us to show our ass in here, what's your excuse?" Casanova approached another stripper and said, "I'd sure like a little pussy." "So would I," she replied, "mine's as big as a bucket."

All the drinks Casanova ordered were more expensive in this particular place than he was accustomed to paying. Casanova was, therefore, in a foul mood. Jimmy the Louse, who was recently hired there, came over to clean his table. Louse said, "Thanks for not making fun of this hump on my back. Most people do." Casanova replied, "Is that a hump? Hell, I thought that was your ass. Everything else is so high in here."

During the evening Casanova was introduced to three women at a near-by table. By this time he was completely wasted. His statement to the first woman after his introduction was "I shore would like to fuck you in the ass". Whereas this is something you might expect to hear in prison, it was completely ineffective as a pick-up line or a favorable impression maker.

When this crude comment failed to get a positive response, he told the second woman, "You'd be alright if you'd loose some weight and get rid of your bitchy disposition". His comment to the third woman was, "would you fuck for a buck or waller for a dollar?" This was not one of Casanova's better nights for conquest. However, one can see why he had so many fights while liquored-up.

Dr. Feelgood sometimes had a few drinks in a local tavern a few miles from town. He and Casanova began to drink together and the topic of conversation generally got down to women. Feelgood's wife was "frigid", among numerous other things and Casanova would counsel the doctor about improving his romantic technique. "What you need," Casanova explained, "is to create some excitement in your sex life. We need to apply some "adaptus fornicatus" to your program. The next time you have sex try this. Tie a string to one of your toes. The other end of the string should be tied to the trigger of your shotgun. Place the gun just outside your bedroom window. When your wife is at a state of orgasm, pull the trigger. This should cure your problem!"

A few days after Casanova saw the doctor at the bar. "How did the "adaptus fornicatus" turn out?" Casanova asked. "Not so well," Feelgood admitted. "I shot the nuts off of the neighbor's dog and my wife shit all over the bed." "This calls for drastic measures," commented Casanova. "First you get her drunk, so she will be persuasive. Tell her what you are doing as you go along with the game. She'll like that! Dress up in a batman suit and tie her up to the bed naked. The last thing you do is blindfold her and tell her you're going to jump off the dresser on to her and the bed. She should get off on all that."

Feelgood was able to get his wife intoxicated enough that she obliged him in this endeavor. All went well until he leaped off the dresser in his batman suit. Unfortunately the doctor forgot about the ceiling fan. The fan was running on high speed and caught Feelgood right between the eyes. Now we have a situation! The good doctor was laid-out cold on the bedroom floor in a batman suit. The wife, who was blindfolded, doesn't know where he went. After sufficient time has passed she began to panic and started to scream for help. Neighbors hearing the commotion broke in to find a naked, blindfolded woman tied spread-eagle on the bed. Feelgood is unconscious on the floor wearing a batman suit, with his "crank" hanging out.

This story spread like wildfire and actually helped the doctor's practice, even though it didn't seem to help his marriage at all. Casanova's counseling of the doctor involved his many exploits which were extremely numerous and varied. The doctor's experiences were usually on the negative side of things. For example, when the doctor was single and struggling through a time in a wheelchair he began to shoot skeet. It was something he could do in a sitting position. During this activity he met a woman who was out practicing on the shooting range. After practice they had a few drinks together at the bar and ended up in her hotel room. If the doctor hadn't been drinking he would probably had been more cautious and gotten to know her better before getting involved to this degree. On the way to her room she confessed to recently losing over four hundred pounds of body weight. No one would have suspected that when she was wearing clothes.

Feelgood immediately noticed that when the clothes came off, the woman looked very similar to a Shar Pei dog. At this point Feelgood became instantly sober and would have run away if he had been ambulatory. "What did you do?" asked Casanova. "I just had to go through with it," replied Feelgood. Casanova commented, "We all have to do some charity work sometime."

Jimmy the Louse began to see himself as a sophisticated intellectual. He changed his name to J.T. Louse.

He had some very weird ideas that he wanted the local newspaper to print. One of the articles was about devil-worship. The newspaper wasn't about to print that. He had a revolutionary idea about a new tax system. Using this system people would be taxed according to how much gas they expelled in their homes. A "fart meter" made from a compressor gauge would be placed in every family home. The central monitoring station in the center of town would collect all the data and record the frequency and the veracity of all gastric activity. Points of increasing activity would start at the lowest classification and proceed up the scale to the highest level. For example, a small "threep", or a "one-putt-ooze-out" would be worth one point. A "silent-but-deadly" would be worth two points. Progressing higher you would have the "flutter-blast" counting for a three-point effort. Finally, a "fundus-break" would be worth four points, while a "plotcher" (or wet fart) would be a flat zero.

The local paper flatly refused to print any of this, which riled J.T. Louse to no end. He would phone the newspaper. When the editor answered, J.T. would fart into the phone. The editor knew J.T. was responsible, so he would say, "Louse, your voice is improving, but your breath is still the same." J.T. joined a health club in a neighboring town to work off his anger and frustration. However, on his first day, he bit a woman on her ass and was promptly ejected from the premises.

Bandit Hanging told J.T. Louse that there was a sperm bank in the next county that was buying semen and paying big bucks.

Louse began to collect his worthless DNA in a half-gallon mason jar. Collecting this much took a considerable length of time. By the time Louse was ready to go to the bank, his efforts had deteriorated. Even cracking the lid of the jar for any reason would immediately permeate the entire room. On the way to the sperm bank Louse went across some very rough railroad tracks. The half-gallon jar bounced off the car seat and broke inside the car. J.T. shot out of the vehicle. The smell was so bad, the car had to be towed. No amount of replacing, refurbishing, or masking ever got rid of the stench. The car was eventually melted down for the recycling of metal.

Louse never moved out of his parent's house. As they aged and became more helpless, J.T. increased his mistreatment of them. When they could tolerate no more abuse, they involved the legal system to place J.T. in a structured setting. In other words, they had him locked up. Interestingly enough, as soon as his parents felt he had learned his lesson, they began to petition the courts for his release. As soon as J.T. was released, he reverted back to his old abusive ways. This ridiculous back and forth involvement with the courts went on for years.

The Louse parents were apparently hoping the court system could somehow salvage J.T., as they had completely failed as parents. The problem was solved suddenly and completely for all time when J.T. began to compose threatening letters to various town officials. These imaginary transgressions he felt towards leading citizens was his final undoing. Threats in writing, plus his lengthy record of violence, placed him beyond redemption in the eyes of the court. And so J.T. Louse passed into history and was never seen again. His memory is revived only in the telling of these episodes.

Meanwhile, Casanova Goodbody was busily doing what he did best, seduction. He took a new prospect to the movies where he purchased a large bag of popcorn. During the show he placed the bag in his lap and tore a small hole in the bottom of the bag. While his date was deeply engrossed in the movie, Casanova inserted his friendly little dick inside the bag. As the level of the popcorn began to drop it wasn't too long until his date grabbed the "prize" at the bottom of the bag. Popcorn flew everywhere and the date ran out of the theater. Everyone stared at Casanova who just shrugged and said, "I think she saw a rat!"

On one of Casanova's worst nights he regained consciousness from a horrendous drinking spree in a junkyard. He was in the backseat of a wrecked car with a naked woman. This particular woman was so dirty that she was dark brown all over. Upon returning to reality Casanova noticed that the only two clean places on the woman's anatomy was around both nipples.

About thirty-five miles south of Briar Patch on the interstate was a large rest stop. This afforded drivers a place to use the restroom and purchase food and drink from machines. Unfortunately this was close enough to the metroplex to draw perverts and deviants of all kinds to that location. Within the restroom was, what was reported on the internet to be a "glory-hole." According to instructions, a man could insert his privates into said glory hole and receive complete satisfaction from the other side.

On a trip home, Dr. Feelgood, who was almost deaf and blind by this time, stopped at this, "din of sin," to use the facility. He was completely unaware of the places reputation.

While relieving himself in the stall, he noticed what he thought was a very scroungy, bald headed rat emerging from a hole in the wall. Having a strong dislike for vermin, but lacking a weapon, Feelgood decided to kill this creature with his shoe. He slipped off a shoe and grasp it at the toe end to use the weighted heal end as a bludgeon. With all the strength and quickness he could muster, Feelgood gave, what he mistook for the mangy rat, a damn good whacking. Despite his efforts, the doctor doubted he had killed the varmint, as it quickly withdrew and he heard a great commotion on the other side of the wall. Feelgood left the rest stop without further incident, however, he later learned that the place was completely demolished due to the rampant, out-of-control perversions that occurred there. "I wouldn't know about all that," he said, "but they sure had a bad rat problem."

Chapter 15

When all the excitement about the little green man, with the big green dick finally died down, Bookworm sold the dildo to Axel Fender.

Axel had planned a motorcycle trip to the coast and decided to wear the thing on the road trip. He had it sticking out of his pants at a forty-five degree angle, right between the handlebars. He only got away with this because cell phones had not yet been invented. A lot of people in cars did notice it though. The few individuals who did know of this plan of Axel's were surprised at how many strangers saw and remarked about the phenomenon within their hearing.

After the road trip, Axel sold the big green phallic to Billy Bob McKnob. McKnob took the thing to the closest metroplex. During rush hour traffic he positioned himself over the freeway at a crossover street. As the traffic crept by underneath him, he began to wave the thing wildly at motorists. This incident got McKnob arrested rather quickly. He was charged with indecent exposure, which was all the police could make out of it. McKnob was soon released, as he had not actually exposed his real self. Fortunately, the big green dick disappeared and was not seen again. It is now probably hanging over the fireplace mantle of some policeman.

Years earlier after McKnob had done some night fishing, he passed Bookworm's house on the way home. It was Christmas Eve and the sun had not yet risen. McKnob decided to play a trick on Bookworm.

He quietly entered the house and crept into the living room. He then leaned against the wall in a sitting position. Braced at this angle he proceeded to crap on the family's floor. Not entirely satisfied with himself, he also cut off some window curtains with his bowie knife to wipe his ass on. As soon as the sun came up Bookworm ran downstairs to see what he had gotten for Christmas. He saw the enormous pile of crap by the tree along with a torn curtain.

Later, Bookworm was wandering around outside the house when a neighbor boy next door saw him. The neighbor was swinging on his new swing set. "What did you get for Christmas?" asked the neighbor. "I think I got a dog, but I'll be damned if I can find him."

One of Catshit Looney's more notable stunts was his attempt to counterfeit money. He was never arrested, probably because his artwork was too amateurish to be taken seriously. He also turned out some unusual denominations – like his famous eighteen dollar bill. Catshit went down to the local bank and presented his eighteen dollar bill, wanting some change. The cashier asked if he would like six threes, three sixes, or two nines. Catshit was laughed at by the entire bank staff..

Bookworm was doing his chores one day when his dad approached him. His dad said, "Catshit has cornholed one of the local grade school boys and the police are looking for him. If you see Catshit, stay out of his way and avoid him."

Sure enough, Bookworm saw Catshit later that day. Catshit was sitting in a police car with several large officers. He did not look happy to be there. As the story goes, Catshit had told his victim he would show him a "trick" and gave him ten cents to co-operate. He then proceeded to sodomize the boy. Catshit Looney was never seen in Briar Patch again. He was placed in an asylum for the criminally insane. After his exposure to Catshit, the victim was never completely "right" again.

Most people knew Catshit was a time bomb ticking, but nothing was done about it. Much of the blame centered around Bandit Hanging, who provided Catshit with "porno" material for Bandit's amusement. Catshit Looney will be little missed. However, he will be long remembered.

About this time Animal-X and Bunny decided to give their relationship another chance. Animal should have been aware from the start that a woman named "Bunny", with a brother named "Casanova" is somewhat of a red flag. When Animal was a small child in his formidable years, his mother bought him a children's book, *The Velveteen Rabbit*. Although this book was written approximately one hundred years ago it is still very popular today. There is also insight in the book for adults too.

The subject matter was more of a worldview from the prospective of a toy. At night the toys would talk to each other and the toy horse who was much older and wiser than the rabbit said, "If you are loved hard enough and long enough you become real. Of course, by that time you are also

114

very shabby. Your hair will be falling out and your nose will have the paint worn off of it."

In the book the rabbit becomes a real rabbit after the housekeeper throws him in the rubbish. Of course this was after he was completely worn out. The love of a child for all of those years had made him real. For only a child's love is given without reservation. This is not unlike the kind of love that Animal had for Bunny. It is the kind that many look for and few find.

Animal told Bunny that when they were married, "I will love you for all of my life, you and no other. Every moment spent without you is a moment wasted." Animal's love was like a blinding white light, so intense that it could not be looked directly upon. In the fullness of time he came to understand that ordinary humanity lacked the capacity to deal with something that powerful. Only a special individual could receive and give that degree of emotion, and Bunny was simply too shallow, self-centered, and ill equipped for such levels. Bunny, on the other hand, saw marriage as a deal that she might or might not honor, but only until a better deal came along. Her motto was, marry young, marry rich, and marry often. Two more opposite people could not be found. The only thing that Bunny had in common with the Velveteen Rabbit was her name.

When he was divorced from Bunny, Animal vacillated from fits of rage to long bouts of depression. He had a record of "their song." He would get drunk and play it for hours. He eventually wore all the grooves off the record by playing it so much.

Animal would have willingly given his very life for Bunny, but deep down he knew that she would never do the same for him. He could never get her to understand his feeling that only love endures beyond death. For in death, he said, "all strength, beauty, wealth and power mean nothing." The staff of the beggar and the scepter of the king are equal. Death is the great leveler, but he felt that the heart that truly loves never forgets.

Animal had the physical strength of five ordinary men. His extreme sensitivity made this a dangerous combination. With her track record, Animal never truly trusted Bunny this time. Her frequent absences from home, with no explanation, just made things worse. One night Bunny failed to come home at all. Animal hid his car and did not go to work that day. Instead he waited at home for her to appear. Sure enough she walked right in.

"Where the hell have you been? And why didn't you call me?" Animal asked. Bunny just shrugged and said, "I spent the night with a friend." "Well," Animal replied, "Did your friend have a dick like a fence post?" His jealousy and curiosity easily rivaled his sensitivity. Animal hired a private detective to watch Bunny and report what he learned. This should have been sufficient, however, Animal was obsessed with knowing the truth.

Unknown to anyone, including the private detective, Animal hid in the trunk of Bunny's car. He had a spoon in the trunk latch to prevent being locked in. Right on schedule Bunny drove away. Unfortunately for Animal the spoon became dislodged and he was now locked in Bunny's trunk. Bunny picked up her latest man "friend" and headed for a motel, as the private detective observed it all.

During the night the detective positioned himself across the parking lot from the motel room Bunny had occupied. He had his camera all set up for pictures of both of them when they left in the morning. The detective noticed that Bunny's car repeatedly rocked and swayed. This, he noted, was very strange, as there was no wind that night.

When Bunny and her "friend" appeared in the morning the detective was filming like mad and Animal was noisily raising all kinds of hell in the trunk. Not knowing who's in the trunk, Bunny opened it. Animal got out, saw the situation, and beat Bunny's "friend" half to death. Bunny escaped unscathed and Animal has his pictures to remind him to stay away from Bunny and car trunks.

In Bookworm's senior year in high school he asked Crash to go to the homecoming football game with him. When she agreed he was very excited. Bookworm had found an old go-cart frame, which he combined with a cement mixer motor. He had been previously grounded for driving this make-shift contraption over eighty miles per hour on the freeway. It was his plan to pick Crash up in his "car". He had bought a corsage, gotten his suit cleaned, and was counting the minutes until homecoming.

The day of the homecoming game Crash phoned Bookworm to tell him she was ill and just too sick to go with him. Bookworm was very disappointed, but decided to go to the game anyway. Crash must have thought he wouldn't go if she didn't because when he arrived at the game, there was Crash with someone else.

The Worm was completely shattered. When Axel Fender learned of this indiscretion, he decided to take certain measures in Bookworm's behalf. Without consulting Bookworm, Axel prepared a gift box full of shit and mailed it to Crash. There was no return address.

Crash picked up her package and went to eat lunch at the school cafeteria. The lunchroom was crowded when Crash sat down to eat and unwrapped her present.

As soon as she saw the shit, she jumped up, shrieked, and threw the box away from her. Crash should have been more careful because the box and its contents landed on the teacher's table. This completely ruined the faculty lunch and Crash had some explaining to do. Bookworm noticed Crash stopped speaking to him in lab class, but he didn't know why until Axel explained it to him.

The locals often hung out at the gas station. Axel liked to play tricks on strangers passing through town who bought gas there. Axel would wear very loose pants that contained styrofoam in the front thigh area. When a stranger entered the station they would see Axel busily whittling some wood with a pocketknife. When they got close enough Axel would curse loudly to get their attention. He would then savagely slam the knife into his front thigh and leave it there. On one occasion when he performed this stunt, an onlooker threw up everywhere. If a good-looking woman came in Axel would put his hand in his pants packet and follow her movements with his finger. The trousers were so loose and baggy that his finger could easily go across his crotch area. The results looked convincingly real.

On occasion Billy Bob McKnob would get drunk in the metroplex bars. The perverted big city types would perform all sorts of wicked, seductive nasties. One night McKnob was unceremoniously dumped from their car in the heart of downtown. McKnob was roaring drunk and his only article of clothing was a spiked dog collar. This stunt made the metroplex news.

Shortly after McKnob escaped from the "van traveling perverts," he looked up Animal-X, who was having lunch in his favorite metroplex restaurant. "Animal, I've got to talk to you," said Billy Bob. "Well, have a seat," replied Animal. "No, I've got to talk to you privately," insisted McKnob. "I guess we'll have to retire to my office, the restroom," suggested Animal.

Upon entering the restroom and looking around the place, it seemed deserted. "Animal, those bastards tattooed me from head to feet." Ripping off his shirt, his body looked like a restroom wall in its tenth printing. "They fucked me, they fucked me! They held me down and fucked meeeeeeee!!r" shouted McKnob. "You're going to have to help me track them down and kill them." He continued to rant on about how they should torture them first before actually killing them.

Animal finally managed to calm McKnob down enough to get him out of the restroom. On the way out he noticed a pair of feet under one of the stalls. Whoever that is, he's going to have one hell of a story to tell someone, thought Animal.

Billy Bob McKnob also hung out at the gas station. His "talent" was to jump up off the ground, click his heels together, and fart. He accomplished this combination of stunning acrobatic skill to mixed reactions. Bookworm was fascinated with the display. He frequently practiced with McKnob at the station. His timing was never right however, and on one occasion he soiled himself badly.

McKnob carried a small caliber pistol that he usually kept loaded with rat-shot. He was cleaning the pistol one day at the station and Bookworm held up a match between his thumb and forefinger. "I'll bet you can't shoot this match out of my hand," said the Worm. Without hesitation, McKnob blasted Bookworm's hand at point blank range. While Bookworm was busily cussing him, McKnob was heard to say, "You will notice, however, that the match is gone!"

When McKnob went drinking across the state line he always carried his pistol. Because there was always the possibility of a serious confrontation, McKnob armed himself with the standard rounds rather than rat shot. Sure enough one of McKnob's friends got into a fight with someone twice his size. The larger man had McKnob's friend down in a booth and was on top of him working him over badly. Being drunk and not thinking clearly at all, McKnob pulled his pistol and shot the man off of his friend. Unfortunately, the man was killed instantly, however, the coroner couldn't find a bullet wound anywhere on the body. It was eventually discovered through autopsy that the bullet had entered the victim's rectum and gone straight to the heart. Billy Bob did some prison time for this, but was well thought of by the other convicts who all called him "Crack shot"!

After McKnob was released from prison he got drunk and went to a car dealership. Posing as a prospective customer he and a salesman went on a demo-drive. As McKnob's driving became increasingly erratic, the salesman asked, "Where are we going?" McKnob replied, "To eternity." At this point the salesman abandoned the vehicle. McKnob got on the freeway, which started a cross-country police pursuit. The speeds varied from 20 m.p.h. to excesses of 140 m.p.h. Finally at approximately 100 miles from the dealership police shot out all four tires and McKnob was returned to prison.

When McKnob was again released from prison he was quite elderly. Most of his rowdiness was behind him at this point. He still got out quite a bit and was seen across the state line frequenting various bars. There just happened to be a local bad boy in these bars who took an immediate dislike to McKnob. The bad boy in question had extensive arrest records himself, mostly minor assault charges. He had never had a serious enough crime to get him incarcerated. He didn't use weapons to beat people with, just his fists! Unfortunately for McKnob, this guy beat up McKnob severely each and every time he saw him.

The bully made a fatal mistake one night when he saw McKnob. He told McKnob he was going to kill him the next time he saw him. The mistake was that he said this in front of witnesses. Later that same evening McKnob entered the diner where the man was eating his meal at the counter. McKnob walked up behind him and calmly shot him in the back of the head with his 44. The badass bully toppled forward into his meal and spoiled a number of people's appetites.

McKnob was no billed and didn't even have to go to court. The police were grateful to finally have this problem person off their hands. When alive, the bully worked on construction, but only enough to keep his strength high enough to hurt people. His former boss was heard to comment, "He told me he had to go back to work for a while because he hit someone yesterday and they didn't fall down."

The man was totally psychotic. He had hurt so many people that one day someone reversed the outcome and gave him a severe beating. On that occasion Mr. Bully was almost beaten to death and was actually left for dead. His recovery required over a month in the hospital because most of his ribs were broken and his face and head had to literally be wired back together. The man did not learn from this however, and upon release from the hospital, returned to his established behavior pattern. Therefore many felt that McKnob had actually performed a public service.

Chapter 16

Firewater Barstool became increasingly more weird and unstable at home, as well as at work. One evening at home he opened the oven door and pissed on the roast that was cooking. This is not something that one ignores. He began "speaking in tongues" and became completely incoherent. When people tried to restrain him he broke away and attempted to "fly" off of the back porch. The hospital staff and doctors were baffled at the cause of this until someone smelled his breath. Apparently Firewater had mistaken a bottle of Lysol for apple juice. He may have had the cleanest intestines in town.

Occasionally, Firewater would pass out or decide to "sleep it off" in a public place. Back alleys or around dumpsters being among his popular choices. He was cured of this behavior by Axel Fender who never forgave Firewater for butchering his Elvis haircut. When Axel would discover the man in this condition he would do terrible things to him. He might take away his shoes and socks. Sometimes he would paint Firewater's fingernails with fingernail polish. The best one was to release a wild rat into Firewater's trousers leg and tie the cuff off at the ankle with twine. This left the only escape route down the other pants leg. Once this happened there was plenty of action! If no rat could be found, Axel would use any wild animal he could find, including non-poisonous snakes.

Watching Ruff Briar's behavior was an eye-opening experience. In the English Middle Ages people went to Mad Houses on weekends to get entertainment from crazy folks. After zoos opened, asylums closed their doors to the public. People then went to see the wild animals, instead of the wild people.

Bookworm's grandmother was fascinated with Ruff Briar's actions and speech. Bookworm spent a good deal of his time at his grandmother's house, but he was terrified of Ruff. The Worm thought Ruff might be a real witch. She certainly fit all the descriptions of witches that he had ever heard about.

One day Ruff came over to the grandmother's house while Bookworm was visiting. His grandmother actually let the "witch" in the house. Bookworm shot out the back door like his pants were on fire. Television was new and Ruff wanted to see one. She knew Bookworm's grandmother had one, so she asked, "Ms. Neill, have you got a vision?" "What?" the grandmother said. Ruff replied loudly, "A-vision, a-vision, a-vision!" Finally, after a good deal of Ruff's shouting, it became clear that she meant a television.

After Ruff had seen the TV, she followed Ms. Neill into the kitchen where she saw some leftover gravy from lunch still in a skillet. "Ms. Neill," Russ asked, "Can I have that gravy?"

"Of course," said Ms. Neill who turned her back to get Ruff a container to put it in. When she turned back around she was shocked to see Ruff tilting the skillet up with both hands and drinking right out of the iron skillet. Ruff never "missed a beat" and began to tell the grandmother about the time she had to shit in a jug because her sorry husband wouldn't stop the car.

It wasn't long after this that Bookworm learned about masturbation. He thought he had discovered something new! "I wonder if anyone else knows about this," he thought. "Why I could probably make a lot of money teaching people how to do this." Fortunately, his older brother stopped him before he made a total fool of himself.

Before B.O. Sharp's house burned down, he was having a problem with some rats. B.O. wanted to catch the rats – but he didn't want to hurt them! His plan was to release them somewhere far away from his house. B.O. acquired some "sticky paper" for the purpose. Sure enough, the next day there were two big rats stuck on the paper. A neighbor was visiting when B.O. brought the rats and sticky paper outside on the front porch. B.O. pulled the first rat off of the paper, however, all of the rats legs remained on the paper. Horrified at what he had done, B.O. retreated back into the house for some scissors to cut the paper off of the second rat.

When he returned the rats were missing, and so was the sticky paper. The neighbor said, "While you were gone, a big tomcat came by and ate the legless rat. Then he grabbed the other rat, (paper and all), and ran off

124

with it." Somewhere there is a large tomcat having a hell-of-a-time getting a sheet of sticky paper off of his face.

When Bookworm still lived at home with his brother, they occasionally got into trouble together. While the parents were out shopping for food, etc., they decided that it might be fun to turpentine a cat. Neither of them had ever done this before, but they had heard about it and figured they could pull it off. First they caught a cat. (No cat will willingly submit to this.) Then they splashed some turpentine on his asshole. (This burns like the mischief.) At that point the cat is trying to run away from his own ass. Eventually the burn subsides with no actual damage to the cat.

All was going well until they released the cat. In their enthusiasm they forgot something very important. Turpentining cats is best performed outside!

They released the cat in the house. The cat was completely "run-amok ". He was all over everything, pissing and shitting as he went. There was no catching him, although they tried desperately to do so. Finally one of them opened the door and the cat shot out of the house. He had thoroughly anointed everything. Rugs, curtains, tablecloths, bedspreads, chairs and couches. When the boy's parents came home there was the biggest washing on the clothesline that had ever been seen.

After Animal-X's last failure with Bunny, he decided to get some hobbies to take his mind off of things. He took up weight lifting and developed even more massively than ever. He also bought a convertible and began to travel. On one trip he was traveling through West Texas, New Mexico, and Arizona. There are places in these states that are very deserted. One might travel endless miles without seeing another car, house, or town.

It was rumored that if you drove west of Abilene, Texas there was a shortage of women. This shortage was indicated by men dressing up farm animals in women's clothes. It was also reported that sheep were dancing in strip clubs. While driving to Abilene, Animal decided this would be a good time to let the top down on his car and get a sun tan. He disrobed down to his underwear and placed his clothes and his shoes in the trunk of his car. Not long after he had shut the trunk lid, he discovered something really

125

bad. He had locked his car keys in the trunk too, as they were in his pants pocket. What an awful sinking feeling that must have been! Remember, cell phones weren't invented yet!

Animal began to walk along the side of the road. Being barefoot was especially painful on a hot asphalt road. Imagine how this looks. An enormous freak of a man, with a fifty-six inch chest and a thirty-two inch waist is walking down a highway in his undershorts. He tried to get the few cars that passed to stop. Absolutely no one wanted to risk picking up someone who looked like that.

Finally he limped into a town with a gas station. They drove him back to his convertible. But before they did Animal noticed some folks at the station who had passed him by without stopping. "Why didn't you stop for me," he asked. "We thought you were out for a walk," they said. They were obviously afraid to let someone with his appearance in their car.

Animal thought that it would be a major undertaking to get the trunk of the car open. All the mechanic did was get into the back seat and lift the backrest out of place. He then handed Animal his pants and car keys. Incidents like this make a person feel really stupid. It was the second time Animal had an incident with the trunk of a car.

Dr. Feelgood was just lucky he never got locked in his trunk while hiding and smoking.

With Animal's appearance it was easy to get work in the closest metroplex where hard-core gyms were in abundance. He had a stunt that never failed to sign up people who looked like Bookworm. It was most effective on thin guys desperate for self-esteem and confidence. He kept on hand several suits that super heroes of comic book fame wore. He paid some of the most seasoned weight lifters to wear Superman, Batman, and other tight fitting suits. When he got the new prospective client in his office he would say, "As you can see all the super heroes train here. Before we accept you as a member you must sign this paper promising not to use your new strength for evil deeds." By now the client's eyes were bugged out and he couldn't wait to sign his name to a contract.

Another trick used at this gym was to take a plastic tape measure and alter the ones that were used to show your progress. For example an inch or so would be cut off the beginning of the tape that measured your arms and chest. The tape measuring your waist would be stretched. All went well unless the tapes were used for the wrong body parts. Sad for the deception, but sadder for the need for the deception. "Tape happy" people need to realize that measurements change daily simply from water retention.

Chapter 17

Axel Fender owned the biggest Harley Davidson motorcycle that was manufactured.

There was a Hells Angels movie playing in the metroplex. This movie featured Harley motorcycles, which drew motorcycle enthusiasts to the show from many miles away.

Axel took a date to the movie and when they arrived there were dozens of motorcycles parked up and down both sides of the street. As luck would have it, there was a good parking place right in front of the movie house, so Axel parked his Harley there. Upon looking around Axel was pleased to see that his motorcycle was by far the largest and finest machine in sight.

When the movie was over the spectators were super-charged and wired-up to ride their motorcycles. Axel was no exception. He and his date were the first people out the movie door. While other people were exiting the show Axel decided to give them an extra special treat. He was going to make a grand exit on the biggest Harley at the gathering. Axel was busily revving-up his motor, in order to get attention focused on him.

When he was ready to go he asked his date, "Are you ready?" She said, "Not yet."

However, the noise of his motorcycle was so loud, he mistakenly thought she said yes. Axel immediately dumped the clutch and the motorcycle stood up at almost a ninety-degree angle. His date fell off the back of the Harley. She cut her ass on the license place as she fell and bumped her head on the pavement when she landed. Relieved of her weight Axel and the machine performed a "wheelie" and shot across the street. It jumped the curb and the sidewalk. The front wheel was descending at just the right angle to catch and crash through the front door of a shoe shop. Displays of shoes flew in all directions as the motorcycle flew through the building with Axel all the while trying to shut the Harley down. He managed to stop short of the back wall, turned around and re-emerged through the smashed door.

All the movie customers had seen his "performance" and were applauding and cheering wildly. His date was just recovering from her fall. As Axel pulled up to retrieve her, she was rubbing both her lacerated ass and her banged head. Axel, always the showman, said, "Woman, get on and don't say nothing – we're looking good." His Harley had sustained a bent front wheel from the shoe store door. So the ride home was rather "bumpy" to say the least.

His date "chewed his ass" all the way and never rode with him again. Interestingly enough, no one reported the incident or turned over any evidence to the police. Apparently they were sufficiently entertained and Axel never heard anymore about it. The next day the newspaper ran an article entitled: "Downtown Shoe Store Is Ransacked By Vandals." For years afterward, when Axel went to Harley shops, the owners would point at him and say, "You're the one."

When Casanova was in the metroplex he found a "porno" shop where he purchased a "battery powered" dildo. He strapped the thing to the inside of his thigh and went to places that encouraged dancing. When he was slow dancing with a woman he would activate the vibrater and rub it up against his partner. The first time he tried this it frightened the woman and caused her to jump. When she jumped, it dislodged the dildo, which fell out of Casanova's pants leg. The thing continued to vibrate and hop all over the dance floor with Casanova on his hands and knees in hot pursuit. All the dancers moved back to watch this spectacle and the band laughed so hard they had to stop playing.

Later in the evening Casanova dropped by the gym. He was early for the fights, but decided to kill some time there, when the phone rang. The gym owner answered it and said, "Nah, I'm not interested in anything like that – here, talk to Casanova." When Casanova took the receiver the voice said, "I'll give you a hundred dollars to beat the shit out of me." Naturally, the violent natured Casanova responded, "Your place or mine." The voice said, "I'll meet you at 'such-and-such' street and we'll discuss it."

There was a pro-football player standing near-by who had heard the exchange. He said, "I'd like a piece of that action too." So Casanova replied, "Well, come on, I'm driving." They arrived at the street address and began to wait for the "employer". During the wait the pro-ball player began to get nervous. "I'll bet this is some karate expert that's going to kick our ass," he theorized. "I'm going to leave." Some time later a rather frail emaciated man appeared. "Are you Casanova?" he said. "Well, let's go to my place. I've got everything there that we need."

After they arrived at the man's house he explained the rules of the job to Casanova. Casanova was to chase the naked man through the house, catch him, and tie him to the bed. At this point Casanova was to beat him with a pre-prepared, handle attached, coat hanger. This was to continue for a specified time. Sessions were usually about thirty minutes. "If I ask you to stop, it just means I want more," the perverted man reminded him.

Casanova was also instructed not to strike the man on the hands, face, or neck. He couldn't afford to have questions asked at work about anything unusual looking. Also, he would have to stand up at work for several days after a session, as it would be impossible for him to sit down. Oh yes, one more thing, Casanova had to wear a chicken suit during the session. Well, just how bad do you need a hundred dollars? Fortunately for the man, Casanova liked violence. He didn't much care for the chicken suit, but as long as no one saw him – what the hell!

The bizarre behavior occurred infrequently at first, but later sessions became so frequent that the "beatee" had to lower the price to fifty dollars instead of one hundred. There was a bonus incentive if Casanova would talk "dirty" or make "chicken noises" while beating him. Although the money was good, Casanova's shoulders began to wear out. It was amazing how tired one's shoulders could become from swinging a coat hanger for thirty minutes.

Eventually, even Casanova began to feel guilty about this behavior. He asked the man why they were doing all of this. The response was "as a child I was never disciplined. Now I can afford it and I want it".

"Well, that doesn't explain the chicken outfit. What's the deal about it?"

"There was a mean rooster at my grandparent's house. It would chase me and jump on me. That was my only physical punishment, ever." The "beatee" was also a "food freak". He asked Casanova to invite a group of his friends over to the chicken man's house for a meal. Dinner was served

on paper plates. After everyone left, Chicken Man would pile the dirty dishes into the bathtub. He would then take off all his clothes and wallow on the dirty paper plates. He would squeal and holler the people's names who had eaten off said plate until he was thoroughly covered in scraps and smears of food.

Casanova said, "And we thought we had problems!" Casanova convinced the food freak, chicken man to see a psychiatrist. Casanova's loss of income paled into insignificance compared to the guilt of continuing this absurd perversion. A few days later Casanova received an angry phone call from the psychiatrist about his patient. The doctor demanded to know what Casanova had been doing to his client. However, nothing came of it and, as time passed, Casanova assumed all the problems were over.

Then one day, quite unexpectedly, he got a phone call from the Chicken Man. "I'm sick of listening to that doctor," said the man. "Why don't you come over and beat the shit out of me again?" By this time even Casanova knew not to go.

There was a tent revival on the edge of town one summer. Axel waited until the congregation was in full swing. At this point he got a stray dog and put shaving cream all around the dog's mouth. Just before he shoved the dog through the tent door he put turpentine on the dog's ass and shouted, "Mad dog – mad dog!" The dog's rear end burning like fire caused the animal to seek help from anyone available. To the people in the revival, it looked like a mad dog was attacking them. The preacher abandoned the pulpit, the choir scattered and the congregation fell down and climbed all over each other in the wild attempt to escape. People poured out the door, crawled under the tent wall and some made "new doors" in the sides of the structure.

When Axel was called up for the draft he decided to beat the odds. He had known people who got out by using some severe measures. For example, he knew a guy who shot his big toe off and was not drafted. He also knew another man who had all his teeth pulled. However, this person flunked the physical because of flat feet! What a waste of good teeth!

Axel decided to make the draft board think he was crazy. With this in mind he worked in the hay field for one month in the same clothes and never washed them. This was his attire on draft board day. He also appeared with a "pet" loaf of bread following him on a string. After eating the mental exam test papers he was asked to leave.

Chapter 18

Boscoe Badass received an inheritance and was able to move out of his country shack. He stayed with relatives in town until the estate was settled. The relatives had a television set. This was a novelty for Boscoe. He spent a good deal of his time watching it and planned to get one of his own as soon as he was moved into his new place.

One day there was a shampoo commercial on the TV. This shampoo was now in a squeeze tube instead of a bottle. His comment was, "Well their toothpaste ain't worth a damn." His daughter said, "That company doesn't make toothpaste!" It appeared that Boscoe had been brushing his teeth with shampoo for some time. Despite these new "town experiences", Boscoe was determined to adjust. He bought a large house in a good part of town. It had indoor plumbing and there was no outhouse on the property.

To everyone's amazement, Boscoe married Ruff Briar and they both moved into their new home.

In the 1940's Briar Patch had dirt streets. When it rained those streets became very muddy. Ruff's first husband would walk to the end of the town's sidewalk during the rainstorms and shout for Ruff to bring him his overshoes. Their shack was about two blocks from the town's sidewalk and everyone could hear them shouting. Ruff would yell back at him in colorful language filled with obscenities. However she always brought the overshoes to him, cursing loudly all the way to town. He would put on the shoes and they would exchange superlatives with each other all the way home. This was a never-ending source of amusement to the residents and store owners.

In the 1950's Briar Patch had improved to gravel streets. Ruff's husband had been killed by this time in the memorable "hoe" fight with another nutty neighbor.

Apparently Ruff had some "normal" relatives. They simply chose to avoid Ruff unless absolutely necessary. One day Ruff's sister came to visit her. The sister appeared to be normal in every way. She drove up to Ruff's place in a very nice car. She was well dressed and well spoken. There was a preschool little girl with her. Bookworm's grandmother, Mrs. Neill, observed all this and decided to go over and meet the sister because if Ruff died no one would know who to contact. It also seemed the neighborly thing to do since she lived so close. Mostly, however, it was because she was fascinated by Ruff and she also possessed a large share of "nosiness."

It seems that Ruff's mother had died and the sister was there to tell Ruff about it. Ruff began to lament her mother's passing by shouting, cursing, dancing about and throwing her arms in the air. At this point the little girl accompanying Ruff's sister looked up at Mrs. Neill and began to giggle. All this was too much for Mrs. Neill. She could barely keep from laughing and hurriedly excused herself, as it would be bad taste to laugh at Ruff's behavior at such a time.

Even after she got home she laughed about the situation for a very long time.

No one could believe Boscoe had married Ruff. Apparently his eyesight was even worse than people imagined. Axel was heard to comment, "Loneliness must be a terrible, terrible thing." Boscoe made Ruff clean herself up. She had regular baths and combed her hair. He stopped her from going to town and making a fool of herself. However, Boscoe's eyesight was very poor and one day Ruff escaped. She went to town, made her old rounds and stopped at all the places that interested her. She saw Mrs. Neill in town that day and stopped to talk to her.

"Mrs. Neill," she said, "you ought to see that damn house I'm a-livin' in. It's got water comin' out of pipes too. One side is a cold as ice and the othern' is as hot as hell! Ma new place has some Goddamn neighbor dogs that keep me up a-barkin' all night long. They come round ma new house a-diggin', a-scratchin', and a-shittin'. Ma new man is gonna run over all of 'um first chance he gets. You'll see 'em a-hangin' on fence posts."

Boscoe's bad eyesight continued to get him in trouble. He went to a neighboring town to buy groceries and upon returning to his car discovered four boys sitting in it. This angered him immensely. He pulled out his old hog leg 45, pointed it at them, and stuttered, "You little ba-a-astards. Get your little a-a-asses out of my car!" All four youths got out and ran away. While loading his groceries Boscoe noticed a football in the back seat and a lot of papers that wasn't his. He realized that it wasn't his car. After finally locating his real car Boscoe drove to the local police station to explain what he had done. The desk sergeant laughed and laughed, "Do you see those four boys at the desk over there? They reported that some crazy old man just commandeered their car at gun point."

By the 1960's all the streets in Briar Patch had improved to asphalt. The street in front of Ruff's old shack remained gravel for a while longer, since Ruff paid no taxes. This was also the decade in which Ruff married and moved "up-town". It was during the 60's that Ruff and Boscoe moved to a larger city some distance south of Briar Patch. Their memory lives on to this day in the minds of Briar Patch senior citizens who were at that time Bookworm's age.

In the years following, Ruff's house became the local dog pound. All stray dogs were housed in the shack. This practice continued for some years until the house was considered too run down for even such an enterprise. Soon after the dog removal, the property was visited once more by that greedy county tax man. He nosed around, looking for something to tax, in order to finance those capitalistic dogs squatting in the school systems. Unfortunately, all he got for his trouble was thousands of fleas infesting his person. All the locals knew not to go on that particular property, but no one bothered to warn him. In the fullness of time, the house of Ruff collapsed into total ruin, the last remnant of which there remains no trace today.

The mayor of Briar Patch, the Honorable Amos Tucker, had aspirations of social climbing in the nearby metroplex. He began to frequent dinner theaters, operas, and join supper clubs in an attempt to meet the right people. His efforts had so far earned a nodding acquaintance with influential socialites. All this came to an abrupt halt when Ruff and Boscoe reappeared unannounced. The mayor was attending a gala event at the Ritz Hotel. It was very formal with tuxedos and all the trimmings. He was in the lobby with all of the other important people, when someone shouted at him from a balcony, "Amos Tucker, you mother fucker!"

It was Ruff and her new husband Boscoe. They ran down the stairs, shouting and cussing, all the way. "We're so goddamn glad to see another son-of-a-bitch from Briar Patch!"

Now that these two had some money, they might resurface anywhere. Nowhere and no one was safe from their antics.

Mayor Tucker was unceremoniously dragged to their suite where Boscoe's two younger brothers were engaged in a brawl. The two brothers in question were named Dallas and Houston. No one knows why they had these names. Perhaps they were conceived in these cities. Dallas and Houston fought a lot as do the two cities.

Ruff and Boscoe chose to ignore the chaos and destruction around them. They simply salvaged some overturned furniture for themselves and their guest. They sat and talked while the fight raged around the room. Both Ruff and Boscoe had attempted to "dress-up" for the occasion. Their clothing choices were tasteless and garish. Ruff's attire looked like some configuration made out of window drapes, while Boscoe sported a shiny suit that was probably material from a sofa. Mayor Tucker was wondering just how much ground he had lost from this incident. He assumed it might possibly be irretrievable.

While Bookworm still lived at home he found and raised a baby raccoon for a pet. The word raccoon is derived from the American Indian word "racanon", which means "clever hands". Anyone who has ever owned a coon knows they can open almost any lock and certainly know how to get into cabinets and drawers. Coons and bobcats both make good pets until they become about a year of age. At that time their hormonal development causes them to become unpredictable. At this stage of development, wise people generally release them into the wild.

Bookworm's coon was still less than a year old when he first brought it into the house. Coons, by nature, seek food in shallow water. Crayfish, clams, minnows, etc. make up the bulk of their diet. Bookworm wasn't paying close attention to the coon as it wandered into the bathroom where his dad was taking a shower. There was shallow water just behind and under those shower curtains. The coon, who had never seen naked human feet, saw a bunch of pink, wiggly things in the shallow water. To a coon, these things we call toes, looked very good to eat. In fact he was sure he had to have them. The family shower was made of sheet metal and made a lot of noise if jumped around in. The coon grabbed and bit those pink wiggly things. Bookworm's dad began dancing and cussing loudly and the shower boomed like a cannon. The coon shot out of the shower with the dad chasing him though the house.

Unknown to Bookworm's dad, his wife was hosting a bridge party for her friends in the living room. In the middle of their card game, a coon, followed by a wet, naked man, streaked through their midst. The naked man was completely oblivious to them, as he cussed and bellowed while chasing the coon. Bookworm and the coon both became scarce commodities for some time after that.

Bookworm's mom also had some rather harsh things to say to his dad as well, regarding the incident. Bookworm shouldn't therefore have been surprised that his parents wouldn't let him keep the guinea pig he brought home after the "coon incident". Guinea pigs are rodents that were domesticated about the same time as the llamas were in South America. Cortez was amazed at the numbers of them that swarmed about the houses of the peasantry. During that era South American Indians used guinea pigs for food.

Not wanting to give up his new pet, Bookworm decided to keep the guinea pig on the church bus. On Sunday, when the bus was used, Bookworm removed the guinea pig and the food and water bowls. All went well until the guinea pig droppings began to build up and started to stink. People were certain that the bus was infested with rats. Traps and poison were put out and Bookworm, not wanting the guinea pig killed, gave it to B.O. Sharp.

Living at the edge of town allowed Bookworm's family to do some limited farming. They had a large hog on the place that had developed a very bad habit. The hog had acquired a taste for "chicken sushi". Any chicken unlucky enough to stray into the pig pen could easily become dinner for that hog. The family had tolerated it so far, because the hog was worth a lot more money than the few chickens he ate. Still it was frowned upon, because chickens did, after all, lay eggs and had value too.

One evening the family was having dinner when they suddenly heard a chicken squawking. The father was tired from working all day and wasn't in the mood to have his meal interrupted over such an incident. He told Bookworm, "Go out there and stop that damn hog from killing my chickens." Bookworm didn't like this job, but was stuck with it. One had to be careful around the old hog, or they might find themselves in the chicken's place, as the prey.

Sure enough, the hog had caught a chicken. Thinking quickly, Bookworm grabbed a rock and threw it at the hog as hard as he could. The rock hit the hog right between the eyes. He had saved the chicken all right, but the hog fell over on its side, stone cold dead.

Being in no hurry to get in trouble, Bookworm decided not to tell more than was absolutely necessary.

He returned to his meal and when his dad said, "Did you stop the hog from killing my chickens?" Bookworm simply replied, "Yes, I did!"

Bookworm's
Dad

Chapter 19

When Casanova still lived at home, his parents went on vacation and he found himself home alone with no supervision. "I'll throw a party," he thought! A large number of people were invited and plenty of alcohol was available. The party was a front yard affair, but was held at night to attract less attention. Casanova became so excited about the success of this gathering that he began to drink long before the guests arrived. In fact he became so carried away with this, that he passed-out cold in the yard before anyone showed up.

He awoke the next morning in the exact position and place in which he lost consciousness.

The sun was just up, birds were chirping in the trees, and people passing on the sidewalk were staring at him. All the drinks and alcohol were gone. Paper cups, empty bottles, and cans, littered the entire yard. Trampled grass and footprints were all around him. He had missed the entire party. "Well," he said, "I guess everybody had a good time." Later that day he discovered someone had painted his toenails with pink polish while he was unconscious.

One of Casanova's ploys to find out if he was wasting his time, or not, with a female companion was his "acid test". This particular practice was only successful now and then. No one knows the exact percent of failure that went with his method. However, it was thought to be high. At night Casanova would park his car in some secluded place while on a date. He would make some excuse to get out of the car for a minute or two. While out of the vehicle, he would completely disrobe. Upon re-entering the vehicle he would immediately press his attentions upon his female companion. Interestingly enough, this "ploy" actually worked on occasion, even on a first date.

In later years, Casanova got a job at a cabinet shop. His boss had contracted a big job out in San Francisco. Casanova and his crew were sent out to do the actual work. They were looking for the address in the downtown area of the city. While crossing the street, they were abruptly swept off the curb by a parade. This wasn't just any parade. It was a gay parade. There were "chicks with dicks" and "dikes on bikes". It took several blocks for Casanova and his crew to extract themselves from the mass or participants. By the time they did, the event had been televised. Casanova's boss and everyone in Briar Patch had seen the crew in San Francisco leading the gay parade. The man could always find a silver lining in every cloud. His comment was, "If some guy sees me in a car with his wife, he won't suspect anything now!"

He would comb through all the newspaper adds in the personal section, and would respond to almost anything. One of his choices to contact was this example:

Woman, evicted! Living in a car with twenty-two dogs. Seeking man.

Age and race is not a barrier.

Hoping to meet new women, Casanova enrolled at the local college. He took a night course called "the occult." The instructor was going over a chapter on spirits and ghosts. He asked the class, "How many of you think you have ever seen a ghost?" A few hands were raised. Then he asked, "How many of you have spoken to a ghost?" Only two hands went up. Finally he asked, "How many of you have had sex with a ghost?" Only one hand went up! "Mr. Goodbody," said the instructor, "you mean to tell me you have actually had sex with a ghost!" "Oh, I'm sorry," replied Casanova, "I thought you said a goat!

This man had actually been thrown out of a whore house for demanding a discount from a prostitute with only one tit.

Casanova was in and out of marriages like a revolving door. He had recently re-married and was attempting to make a favorable impression on his new family. One of his latest wife's relatives had died and Casanova had agreed to act as a pallbearer. He and his latest missies were driving to the funeral when Casanova got into a running "pissing match" with another motorist. One of them had done something in traffic that annoyed the other one. Both were shouting and making suggestive gestures at each other while driving on the freeway. Casanova dropped his pants and stuck his ass out of the window. Following that he pulled out a pistol and displayed it to the other driver.

At this time in history, cell phones had been invented and the other motorist had one readily available. The next thing Casanova knew, local police and highway patrol cars were all around him. He was pulled off the road and was being handcuffed when the new wife's family drove by. Everyone saw him! There was, therefore, one pallbearer missing at the funeral. Everything turned out all right though. It seems that the deceased had one leg amputated. Without Casanova on the missing limb side, the load was still properly balanced.

Tired of living in the boarding house, B. O. Sharp and Animal-X decided to rent a house a few miles outside of town. B.O. was anxious to go into the skunk business in a large way and Animal-X was still despondent from the failed marriage. He had plenty of time on his hands with nothing better to do. They built numerous skunk cages and obtained a U.S.D.A. Fur Bearers License in order to conduct business legally. All this seemed to keep Animal-X's mind occupied.

When December rolled around, large numbers of skunks were out at night looking for each other, since this was skunk breeding season! Skunks have poor eyesight and do not run very fast. They don't need a lot of skills because they have no natural enemies. In fact, the only thing that prevents them from over-populating the earth is their bite. Skunk bites are "toxic" to other skunks. During the mating season the males fight and bite each other. This keeps the population in check, but also gives rise to the notion that many skunks carry the disease "rabies". Because all skunks are nocturnal, the only rabid skunks would be "day visible" ones.

The best way to catch skunks is with a large dip net attached to a ten-foot handle. Once the skunk is scooped up in the net, he can't plant his feet to aim his shot. Quickly grab the base of the tail and point the rear end away from you. (This is a good time to threaten any companions that owe you money.) Deposit the skunk in a metal or plastic trashcan. Make sure the lid is secure. Skunks can "shoot" out the top of a lidless can and a wire cage would not suffice at all.

One should remember, one skunk to one can, to prevent biting. The best place to hunt skunks would be in the country. Simply drive around gravel roads slowly at about midnight with a powerful searchlight scanning the fields. This can be problematic as Animal and B.O. discovered. There is an illegal activity called "spotlighting". An animal will "freeze" when looking into a powerful beam of light and becomes easy prey for hunters who practice this.

Animal and B. O. were out searching for skunks one night when the police stopped them. Apparently someone had seen the spotlight and reported it. Since they hadn't caught any skunks yet, they looked suspicious. Once the two got out of their pickup truck and the police got a good look at their size, things got worse. Animal-X could pass for a sasquatch and B.O. resembled a gorilla. Both officers had their coats pulled back and one hand on their pistols. They were convinced that Animal and B.O. were hunting.

"Where's your guns?" they asked! "We don't have any," Animal said. "What's under your coat?" they asked B.O. "My belly," he answered! A search of the pickup and both suspects revealed no guns. The police were skeptical of the real facts until Animal gave them one of his business cards. It read: Polecat Mountain, Fuzzy Skunk Farm – with the usual additional information. Both officers just looked at each other. They were convinced at last.

The remainder of the night proved to be a profitable one. Although Animal and B.O. looked around for the same policemen to show them their catch, they could not find them. They phoned an old trapper named "Lonesome Claud" about thirty-five miles away. Claud was a gravedigger by day and a trapper by night. The funeral home gave him the wooden boxes that coffins were shipped in. He used these boxes for cages. The lower half of one of Claud's ears was missing and his arms carried more scars than hair. Trapping and handling animals had left their marks on him.

Claud said that since the wind was out of the right direction that night, they could do business. If, however, the wind was wrong he would have to wait because there were neighbors on one side of his property. Animal-X and B.O. had never seen skunks de-scented before, but figured once they observed it, they could do as Claud did.

Claud had a huge circular metal watering trough about one hundred yards from his house. He insisted on operating at that location. The metal trashcans were unloaded and the fun began. Neither Animal-X nor B.O. knew what to expect, but whatever it was, they got a real education that night. Claud took off the trash can lid. By this time the skunks all had an overnight rest and plenty of time to replenish their ammunition. Claud looked in the can and the beady-eyed skunk fuzzed up and looked back.

For a "pear shaped" man, Claud was extremely quick. He dove into the can, head first, all the way up to his waist. Then he quickly re-emerged holding the skunk away from him by the base of the tail. Skunk spray was flying and people were running. The operation was simple and quick. However, there were eight more trashcans to go. Claud was successful in eight out of his nine attempts that night. In one of the contests of quickness, the skunk won.

Claud was a fraction of a second slow and the skunk got him point blank in the face. "That's when we found out what the stock trough was for," B.O. said. Claud abandoned the skunk in the can and dove into the water tank like a big bullfrog. After some time Claud re-emerged and finished the job. No extra charge. Animal and B.O. de-scented all the baby skunks themselves. The little skunks are unable to spray until they are older. One must not wait too long after they "fur out" and are getting around well.

While in high school, many in the football locker room and showers discovered that Animal was not created equal with most men. All the locals soon knew his "condition", because there wasn't much news in Briar Patch. An eleven-inch phallus would probably place Animal near the top two and one-half percentile on a bell curve. It is amazing how most men and even some women wish that it belonged to them. However, as Animal discovered, it wasn't enough to keep Bunny at home.

When he was in the service Animal developed a friendship with one of the islanders from the South Pacific. Animal promised to visit him after they were discharged. His islander friend would say, "When you come to my country, you'll be famous." After his divorce Animal decided to visit his friend for a week or so. However, he wasn't prepared for what awaited him on the island. Word of his "ga-au", as it is called there, (the word actually translated to horse), has spread all over the island. One hundred and fifty thousand natives were all rabidly anxious to see the big ga-au. Apparently there was less entertainment on the island than there was in Briar Patch. Only a few people there even had television. It was reminiscent of Hawaii four hundred years ago.

The natives were almost "child-like" in their interest of something new or different. They would come around in the evening and ask politely to see Animal's big ga-au. Since he always refused, this only served to increase their curiosity. Larger crowds developed each night and Animal was served endless amounts of alcohol, in hopes he would do an "unveiling". The wily natives arranged for Animal to meet a willing female, (very willing, I might add), at a local celebration. They hid behind rocks and palm trees, hoping for a performance. The woman asked him, "Is it true that you have an eleven inch ga-au?" Animal said, "I don't know where people get ideas like that."

Not easily put off, she arranged to take him home with her. By then, Animal's friends had left him and simply disappeared. Because he didn't know the customs, Animal was afraid of what might happen to him if he stayed with her. He escaped, but was ever watchful and cautious of her reappearance. Not to be put off, the "hosts" brought an inspector from town to inspect his ga-au. He was told it was the custom. By this time Animal had begun to "wise-up" and replied, "Fuck your custom!"

Next they produced a gentleman who had elephantitis in his scrotum. (This is a disease originating from mosquitoes.) It is easily curable. If left untreated however, the victim will eventually have to carry his testicles around in a wheelbarrow with a tarpaulin thrown over them. The man in question had not progressed to that point yet and was still ambulatory.

"We'll show you Jimmy's balls if you'll show us your ga-au," they said. Animal wasn't tempted! "We'll all get naked in the yard together and then you won't be embarrassed" was their next attempt. Animal even refused this innovative offer. On his last day there the crowd had dwindled to two people and he finally relented and showed those two. They first had to promise not to ever ask again.

**Lonesome
Claud**

After he returned home Animal decided to remodel his house. He acquired a large amount of lumber and built an enormous deck on the house. It was in excess of one thousand square feet. One had to be cautious how you phrase and pronounce certain words. If you aren't careful they could sound like something you never intended to say. Crash found this out when she announced at the unemployment office that she and Bunny were "hoers", meaning gardeners. At the local convenience store Animal was waiting to check out with the cashier. Since he knew the checker, he said, "When you get off work, drop by the house and see my big deck." The woman turned red and all the customers in line behind Animal began to laugh. He didn't figure out what was so funny until he was outside with his purchase. By then it was much too late. As I recall, about eight of nine people did actually show up at his residence. He showed all of them the deck, much to their disappointment.

At one time Animal-X's father was in bad health, so Animal checked on the old man frequently. One day he called his dad's house but no one answered. When Animal arrived at the residence he found the doors all locked. Although he rang the bell, knocked and yelled loudly, there was no response. Fearing the worst and starting to panic, Animal kicked the front door off its hinges. The dad had been asleep and was just creeping toward the door to open it when it blew off its hinges and fell on top of him. Animal ran into the house right over the door mashing his father into the carpet. The old man later commented, "Animal was more dangerous than the illness."

There was an additional door incident in which Animal was involved. He had located Bunny's car at a motel in a nearby town. Since he had no way of telling which room she and her "tryst" was in, he devised a unique method of discovery. Reasoning that since the car was in his name and he had paid for it, he should just set it on fire. He drove across the street and watched through his binoculars, as all hell broke loose. Fire trucks arrived and everyone ran out to the parking lot, including Bunny and her companion. In this way Animal got a fix on her room number. After a reasonable amount of time passed the fire trucks left and all of the excitement died down, he made his move.

Seething with righteous indignation, Animal kicked down the door and stormed into the room. Only then did he notice that the room had a squad of police in it taking interrogational notes. Animal did some jail time over the incident and never kicked in any more doors.

Chapter 20

When Animal-X, Axel Fender, and Bookworm were still in high school, some very inappropriate behavior evolved. Their capers tend to verify this. Axel and Animal had just finished a hay-hauling job and had gone to a local lake to clean up and relax. This particular lake was built for flood control and would get deep quite suddenly. A person had only to get in the water a few feet from the shore to find deep water. While relaxing a few feet out, they saw Jimmy the Louse approaching. J.T. was a disagreeable lunatic at best. Soon a verbal confrontation developed.

Being clearly outclassed in a contest of wits, Jimmy dropped his trousers and crapped in his hand. (An act in itself that causes disbelief.) He then threw this handful on Animal and Axel. Axel was hit on the arm and shoulder, while Animal got hit square in the chest. Infuriating the two most athletic people in high school is never wise. They caught J.T. and practically drowned him in the lake. This may have been the only act of discipline the Louse ever received.

Bookworm liked to sneak off into the woods and smoke dried grapevines. A person involved in this practice needs to have a decent knowledge of woodcraft. The Worm accidentally cut a length of poison oak instead of grapevine. Smoking poison oak is a disaster. Not only is your mouth affected, your lungs and throat suffer as well. This one incident cured Bookworm of all desire to smoke anything again.

B.O. didn't get drunk often. This was a very good thing considering his level of strength. He was, however, very drunk one evening at the local drive-in diner. Axel was there too and never liked to be around B.O. when he was intoxicated. As Axel said, "You never can tell what he may do next, and he doesn't know either."

B.O. approached Axel and the others that were hanging out and announced, "I've got to shit!" "Well," Axel said, "Why don't you just shit in your pants?" To his surprise, that is just what B.O. did. It seems that any thought put into his head while drinking becomes his own!

B.O. said. "What now?" Axel just shrugged. At this point, B.O. stepped out of his overalls, grabbed them by the cuffs, and began to swing them rapidly in a circle over his head. Shit flew in all directions and Axel and his friends took cover by ducking behind cars. In the middle of the "shit storm" Bookworm came out the door of the diner and was plastered in the center of his chest. He was wearing his new mohair sweater – so the turd stuck there.

Bookworm ran from person to person seeking help, but everyone ran away from him. Axel decided he should do something for the pathetic Worm – so he grabbed the sweater (it was a pull over) and jerked it over Bookworm's head. Unfortunately the turd rolled right over Bookworm's nose and face, resulting in him immediately throwing up. So much for well meaning acts.

On another occasion Axel was busily attempting to seduce one of Bookworm's family cows. Bookworm was aware of the situation and was giving Axel some privacy in the barn. About this time Animal-X drove up in his hay truck and Bookworm informed him of the situation. Not wanting to miss this scene both boys sneaked into the overhead hayloft to witness this unbelievable spectacle. Axel was chasing the cow with a bale of hay in hand so he could stand on it, to perform. Eventually the cow stopped and all was going well. At this point Animal stood up and yelled at the top of his lungs. The cow took off and Axel finished off in mid-air. All this must have been a "turn-on" for Animal because what happened next surprised everyone. Animal un-limbered his massive weapon, stroked it quickly about a dozen times and accompanied with insane laughter, blew a horrendous load out of the hayloft. All the spectators, including the cow, were stunned into open mouth silence. In later years Animal denied that any of this ever happened.

After graduation Axel, Animal, B.O. and others from Briar Patch (including Casanova) went on the rodeo circuit. B.O. had not developed agoraphobia yet so he was able to travel. They did quite well at rodeo-ing and when the finals were over they all went to Jamaica to celebrate. Jamaica was not a good choice due to B.O.'s resentment to black men and his pig incident. In fact B.O. later proved to be a huge liability while there.

This group got an all-inclusive deal cheap and everything was fine until the first morning when they came down for breakfast. They were informed by the native bouncers that they had to have on a tie to eat in the dining room. Naturally none of them had brought ties, just blue jeans and shirts! Axel tried to explain that they had paid for an all-inclusive package, including meals. No one mentioned anything about ties. The native bouncers were quite unsympathetic as several additional bouncers joined the group.

The Briar Patch crowd was, in general, in a surly mood after being denied food. It was no surprise when Axel announced, "Gentlemen, start your engines." Leading the pack, Axel and the rest plowed into the bouncers like a force of nature. B.O was shouting his war cry, "You fucked my pig, you fucked my pig!" This only served to mark him as the most serious of lunatics and people shied away from him en masse.

The dining room was utterly destroyed, patrons scattered and the police were summoned. The Briar Patch gang was brought before the local magistrate to explain the situation. On the way to the magistrates office Axel attempted "once more" to convince B.O. that all black men did not fornicate with pigs. And please don't accuse the magistrate of this activity. B.O. remained skeptical and unconvinced. But at least he was relatively quiet during the proceeding. You could still hear him grumbling and muttering in the background, "That no pig was safe in this country." Not wanting to hurt the tourist industry, the magistrate put the Briar Patch gang on a local luxury ship with unlimited food, drink, and alcohol. This kept them away from decent "gentlefolk" until their trip was over.

Years later Axel and his entire extended family (about 12 people) took a trip to Disney World in Florida. Axel didn't want to go on this trip and was not in a good mood about the affair.

Upon arriving at the Florida airport they phoned for transportation. Eventually a van pulled up and took Axel and his father back to the rent-a-vehicle center. Axel asked why they didn't bring the whole family since the van could have easily accommodated the entire party.

The Arab owner was busily doing paperwork and saying, "My friend, my friend, this and that."

Axel was being ignored. Naturally a confrontation developed and the Arab cursed Axel's father. Axel, who was by now short tempered, jerked the Arab over the counter and commenced to pound on him when a very large Arab came out of the back. His eyes went straight to the baseball bat in the corner. Both he and Axel went for the bat at the same time, only Axel got there first. He caught the big Arab right between the eyes with the bat and laid him out cold beside the first Arab. There was a lady and a little girl in the rent-a-center also waiting for service. They witnessed the entire situation, but said nothing. They just stared with eyes as big as dinner plates.

Axel tossed the bat aside and said, "Well, I guess we'll have to go across the street to get transportation." While they were doing business across the street Axel noticed some police cars pulling up to the Arabs rental business. He told his Dad, "Maybe we should go back and explain to the police what really happened!" The police were not happy about the situation, however the two witnesses confirmed Axel's story. Therefore he was not incarcerated. The police warned him that he was not welcome in that state and would be arrested on sight if he ever returned.

Axel then moved to a larger neighboring town. He found a house in the suburbs and attempted to remodel it. He also got a job working for the city water department. All was going well until the electrical inspector came by. He informed Axel that the wiring was all wrong and would have to be re-done. He wouldn't tell Axel what was wrong – just that he had to re-do it. So Axel re-did the whole job, only to be rejected by the inspector a second time. The inspector told him that he had to go by the electrical handbook. Axel asked where he could get such a book and was informed by the man that only licensed electricians could have the book. Axel re-wired the house a third time.

The inspector was a rat-faced man who had a plate of metal in his head from some previous accident. Both his eyes stared in different directions, reminding Axel of a lizard. Because the inspector lived only a block or so away it was easy for him to watch Axel's progress and check up on him. The fool rejected Axel's third attempt and would not tell him what was wrong with it. Being unable to resolve this frustrating situation, Axel just lost it!

"You gotcheyed chicken fucker, I'll hit you so hard you'll be talking to dead relatives." That was the last thing the inspector heard before neighbors pulled Axel off the man. He had the inspector down in the yard beating him like a broken drum. Axel was reported to the city for his behavior, but since both men were city employees, nothing was done. The inspector never drove by Axel's house on his way home again.

There were some yard men who came around in a group and did most of the neighborhood yard work. Axel discovered that 80% of Americans hire their yard work done today. The bulk of it is done by illegal immigrants from Mexico. Axel heard his dog barking and raising hell in the backyard. He had on only his boxer shorts at the time. When he slipped on his cowboy boots to step out and see what was disturbing the dog.

There were two of the yard men crapping in Axel's backyard. This angered Axel immensely. He loosed the dog on one of them and descended on the other one cursing them in fluent Spanish. The dog tore into one and Axel began to beat the shit out of the other one (literally). He hadn't been back in his house long before the police arrived. Apparently such behavior did not go unnoticed by the neighbors. Axel explained to the officer what happened.

The policeman asked, "Why didn't you just call us?" Axel said, "Hell, by the time you got here they would have wiped their ass on a Wendy's sack and been gone."

The police said, "Well, they come here informally, so what can you expect!" Axel sold the house and moved back to Briar Patch.

One day his motorcycle caught fire while sitting by the curb in Briar Patch. They were able to extinguish the blaze but the machine was severely damaged. While people were surveying the damage Firewater Barstool happened to stagger by on the sidewalk. Apparently he had been drinking his hair tonic again, because he thought he was seeing an "organ grinder". "Hey Buddy," he said, "You may not be getting a hell-of-a-lot of music out of that thing, but you're sure burning the piss out of your monkey."

The leading matriarch of the creature clan had just finished her specialty, "a rat pie"! She sat the pie on the table to cool and when she returned to the table someone had gouged a handful of the corner of the pie. Calling all the adolescent creatures to the table she said, "Who put their fingers in my pie?" No one would admit the offence so she said, "If the guilty person doesn't tell me who did this I'm going to whip all of you."

The baby creature who could barely walk and talk spoke up and said, "Me did it! Me like-um rat pie!" Well, no one thought he could even reach the table, but apparently if he stretched and got up on his toes he could just reach the pie. Everyone thought it was so amusing that no one was disciplined for the offense.

People were always leaving "care packages" for the Creature family. One gift was a gift of paper plates. Since the Creatures all eat with their hands, wiping the grease off on thighs or loincloths, they had no need for forks, plates, and so forth. In fact they didn't know what to make of the strange stuff in the box. They eventually decided they could use them for chamber pots. On a cold night they would crap in one, then cover it with another one turned upside down. When the house accumulated a sufficient pile, the load was then dumped elsewhere.

Bookworm had a deaf cousin who sometimes visited the family. This particular relative was fascinated with R.J. (the dog's) testicles. When R.J. was lying on the porch the cousin would flop the "nuts" from side to side. One day he decided to twist R.J.'s nuts. On the first revolution R.J. put up with this, but on the second revolution R.J. growled at the boy. Being deaf, the warning went unnoticed. On the third revolution R.J. bit the offending nut twister on the face. So never twist a dog's nuts beyond two revolutions, they simply have no tolerance beyond this point. A dog is just not a wind-up toy.

When Bookworm was in the first grade he had a traumatic experience. For some unknown reason he lost control of his bowels in the classroom. As everyone was seated and studying, he thought, "Maybe no one will notice or be the wiser. Perhaps I will get away with the indiscretion." Unfortunately he was seated next to the wall. In this wall was the heating system that blew heat across the room. Within a few minutes the classroom smelled like a sewer. No matter how innocent Bookworm looked and acted, the smell was traced directly to him. He was immediately sent home in disgrace. The worst part of all this was having to walk several miles with his pants full of crap.

Casanova was looking forward to going to a special party when his stomach began to act up. It was discovered that he had some stomach ulcers and would be unable to drink alcohol at the forth-coming event. Partying without alcohol was an unforgivable situation to Casanova. He therefore devised this solution to the dilemma. Since alcohol goes directly into the blood stream through the stomach wall, he reasoned that he needed only to by-pass the ulcered area of his digestive tract. Just before the party he took a fifth of vodka with a fleet (portable) enema; and (for those of you in Eastern Oklahoma, it means he hosed it up his ass!) The results were the same effect that taking alcohol in the more traditional form would accomplish. In short, Casanova was high as a kite with no damage to his ulcer. This method deprives the user of tasting however, as there are not suppose to be taste receptors located in that area. It was also suspected that this practice could really burn a person's ass.

160

Chapter 21

When Bookworm was quite small (preschool), he spent a good deal of his time at his grandmother's house while his parents were at work. His grandmother was a large bear of a woman resembling a white version of Hattie McDaniel, or "Mammy" in the classic movie, Gone with the Wind. Ms. Neill felt vulnerable to no one except possibly sales people. The woman had absolutely no sales resistance. She felt sorry for the people forced to go door-to-door in order to make a living. She always bought their wares even though she didn't want the merchandise. Turning them away was very unpleasant for her. She would often hide until they went away.

When Bookworm was at her house she would suddenly grab him and hide in the attic or the bathroom until the sales person went away. "Why are we hiding?" he would ask. "Be quiet, there's an agent at the door!" she would say. Bookworm didn't know what an agent was, but it must be fearsome indeed, because Ms. Neill wasn't afraid of anyone. Bookworm eventually became "conditioned" to hide from any stranger that came to the door.

One day a strange man came to the door and just walked right in the house. "My God," thought Bookworm, "One of them has actually penetrated the house!" The boy immediately dove under a chair to hide like a dog. "What's the matter with that kid?" said the uncle who had just come home. Bookworm's mother said, "Oh, Mom has taught him to hide from sales people. He must think you're one of them." Everyone had a good laugh at the boy's expense.

Adult conversation was sometimes confusing to Bookworm. Adults would talk about some man getting fired and laugh about it. How could being set on fire be a laughing matter? One of Bookworm's favorite "tricks" at this age was to repeat "bad words" he would overhear back to the adult that said them. He got his start at this when his grandmother mashed one of her fingers. "Shit!" she said.

Not knowing Bookworm was hiding nearby. The boy jumped out of hiding, shouting "shit, shit, shit" loudly, and always in successions of three. Ms. Neill thought it was funny and he repeatedly got away with this behavior because the adult had, after all, said it first. One evening he was hiding under the kitchen table waiting for his chance at the "word game". His aunt called someone a "peon". Bookworm jumped out of hiding and shouted it three times. "You can relax," said his aunt, "it isn't a dirty word." Non-residents of Briar Patch usually got a shocking education upon any visitation or exposure to the locals.

Dr. Feelgood was a prime target for salesmen because the doctor obviously had some money. Feelgood detested salespeople. In his own words he said, "I absolutely loathe them." Not everyone in Briar Parch knew what loathe was, but they asked no questions of him. Knowing that Axel Fender was the best prankster in town, Feelgood asked him what he would do to get rid of these pests and have some fun at the same time? The solution to the doctor's problem was readily conceived. Although it was somewhat costly and time consuming, it generated great satisfaction and as the doctor said, "We all had such fun!"

First they rounded up "trick" furniture, and phony glass windows and doors. These were the type used on movie sets and shatter upon impact when someone hits them. The glass is specially made so that it does not cut. Other props were starter pistols from the track department that fired blanks. The staff at the doctor's office also took a brief tumbling course in order to learn how to fall correctly. This would be useful in the fake brawls that were to take place.

Some of the doctor's patients auditioned for roles when the word spread about the undertaking. B.O. Sharp was not considered. He could accidentally hurt someone by mistake. None of Casanova's family was useful because their love of fighting might overcome their logic in the heat of fake battle. Crash turned out to be a superb actress, to everyone's surprise. Maybe it was because she was so close to being schizophrenic in real life. Several "skits" were worked out and everyone waited for the first victim to show up and attempt to sell them something.

Sure enough the very next day a salesman appeared. He was sent in to see the doctor and given about five minutes before Crash burst into the doctor's office in a rage! "Where's my back child support you son-of-a-

162

bitch? You think you can screw me on your fancy desk and toss me aside to take care of your bastard without so much as a by-your-leave?" The doctor replied, "Get out of my office you vile strumpet! I've stepped over better things than you, looking for a place to masturbate!" At this point Crash would scream, pull the blank starter pistol out of her purse, and blast away at the good doctor. Feelgood would pretend to be hit and topple sideways from his chair. Crash would then say, "We don't need any witnesses," and then turn the gun on the salesman. This skit never failed to make salesmen scatter to the four winds.

Another favorite caper required the doctor to assume the role of a homosexual. Not knowing how to act gay, Feelgood had to consult one of his patients, who happened to be of that persuasion. Briar Parch didn't have any gay people, as far as anyone knew! The doctor's patient was from out-of-town. He used this office to conceal any evidence that might slip out and damage him at home. It seems that this particular patient had contracted hepatitis on three separate occasions from "eating assholes." The doctor said, "You have had hepatitis three times now. Your liver won't take a fourth round of this. I am therefore taking you off all assholes permanently! No more 'rimming' for you." This is apparently what it is referred to in the gay community. Feelgood got a very thorough education on gay behavior from this patient.

If Axel was in town when a salesman dropped by the office, they would use their "gay act"! After the sales person was admitted to the office Axel would kick down the doctor's door and they would both become flaming drag queens, lisping at each other and talking in high-pitched female voices. Both would "come out of the closet." Axel would say, "You wanton hussy, you've diddle our Chinese houseboy behind my back. This is the thanks I get for giving you the best years of my life." The doctor would respond, "Shut up you silly bitch! You can just eat a meat Popsicle!" Axel would then grab Feelgood and throw him through the outside fake glass window onto a trampoline set there for this occasion. With the doctor gone the salesman would promptly leave.

Sometimes the entire office staff would have a "free-for-all", breaking furniture and rolling on the floor. If the salesman tried to intervene or break up the fight, everyone would suddenly turn on him and he would be running for his life.

The staff also kept on hand a supply of spoiled produce from a local grocery store. In this instance the salesman and his vehicle would be unmercifully pummeled with all sorts of rotten eggs, vegetables, and assorted fruits. Numerous tales began to circulate about the crazy doctor at Briar Patch. This cut down on sales people sharply and surprisingly enough did wonders for the doctor's practice. It appears that the patients in Briar Patch suffered from boredom and hoped to be at his office the next time a salesman came to call.

Chapter 22

The big commercial gyms in the metroplex gradually began to influence certain members of the Briar Patch community, as more and more of them gravitated in that direction. Only a few of these places were hard-core dungeon type gyms. These were "tailor made" for Briar Patch. Occasionally they would workout at a more up-scale place, but only if the equipment was adequate.

There was such a place that was popular, located on the edge of an affluent, old money, rich part of town. A world champion lifter owned it, so it catered to low brows and the elite alike. Axel Fender frequented this gym – because it had "fight night" every Friday when regular business hours were done. Axel began to spend time with one of the women instructors there and it wasn't long until they contrived a plot to scare the local masseuse.

The masseuse was an odd sort of gentleman who took everything entirely too seriously. Axel found a female dummy that he and his instructor companion "dolled up" to look real. After the gym closed for the night they placed the dummy on the masseuse's massage table. They made it look like the female instructor. She put one of her wigs on it and plenty of make-up. The legs were encased in hose and had a pair of her shoes on the feet. A sheet was thrown over everything except for the head and feet. In the center of the chest a butcher knife was sticking out through the sheet. An entire bottle of catsup was splashed over the sheet and wound sight. Even a bloody handprint was on the wall.

Knowing that the masseuse would be opening the next day, they went home and thought how funny he would look when he got to work and saw everything. The plan went even better than they could have ever imagined. The masseuse was somewhat simple-minded and upon witnessing the "murder scene" immediately phoned the police and the gym owner too. The gym owner was sleeping in that day and was not in a good humor for being roused at an early hour.

"Someone killed Becky last night. She's lying on my table with a knife sticking out of her. Get here quick!" said the masseuse. By the time the gym owner arrived the police were already there. Since there had never been a killing in the rich part of town the police were novices at this type of crime scene. They were told not to touch anything until forensic arrived. They had, however, poked their heads into the murder room long enough to see for themselves. Getting out of his car, the gym owner noticed one of the cops throwing-up outside, which seemed to "trigger" several others to follow his example. Soon forensic arrived and went into the crime scene. This was a big deal and the TV camera and news people were all gathered by now. Well, the chief of police was mad as a Jap! It turned out that Axel and the female instructor had informed a desk sergeant that they were doing this stunt, and to stop all investigations as soon as the call came in. Unfortunately, he had taken that particular day off and forgotten about the incident. The gym did a thriving business after the thing was over.

Way down town, in a burned-out slum area was the oldest gym in the state. It dated back to the 1920's and 30's. Not much had changed in this particular place and it had only had two owners during all this time. This gym was so old and seedy that it positively dripped atmosphere. Many movies were shot in it because of its authenticity. Only hard core serious lifters, wrestlers, professional athletes and perverts trained here. In short, it was perfect for Briar Patch people.

Occasionally up-scale business types showed up. One especially memorable one was a sissy little man who wore a three-piece suit and carried an umbrella. He used the umbrella not for rain, but for shade. His type usually didn't last long! There were also some homosexual men who frequented the place. They knew not to touch anyone or the owner, Big Tony, would throw them out.

Apparently one of these guys had been watching people changing clothes through the dry sauna window and had masturbated on the seat area. The sissy little man went into the dry sauna and sat on this moist area, matting all the thick hairs on his ass. He complained long and loud to Big Tony about the situation and people overhearing, began to "mess" with him.

Some fake plastic dog shit was purchased at the magic shop and when the sissy man showed up, they placed the fake dog shit in the shower. With water running over it, the results looked surprisingly real. The victim burst out of the shower with a towel wrapped around him. He went straight to the office.

"Tony, what kind of a place are you running? Someone's had a bowel movement in the shower!" He shouted. Tony and the sissy man went to investigate, followed by many gym members. The two of them, both holding their noses, approached the plastic shit with a long stick. Upon poking the mass it was discovered that its true nature was plastic. The sissy man was thereafter a marked man and soon departed.

The worst homosexual man in the gym was Old Pole, who owned Pole's Hotel down the street. At his mid 90's, he was thought to be the world's oldest living gay man. Pole had what we called a (locker-room membership) since his primary reason to be there was to view naked men. He had two methods that he favored. One was to hide in the dry sauna and peep out the smoke tinted door window. His knuckles and nose tip resting on the glass surface gave away his game. The other ploy was to feign slumber in a dressing room chair. Pole wasn't really asleep, you see, as one eyelid always fluttered as he watched people change clothes. Being overweight and covered in gray body hair, Pole looked like a huge gray louse, or a melted wedding cake deposited in the chair. Occasionally he would make the mistake of getting out into the gym area. The patrons were not always socially correct in this weird setting.

There was an airline pilot who enjoyed exposing himself in public places. He would say anything to anyone, anywhere. "Hey Pole!" he shouted, "Have you sucked any good dicks lately?" Pole would just squeal and dance there in one spot. A sight not soon forgotten! One day the towel man came in the gym while delivering and saw Old Pole. "Do you actually allow this man in here?" he asked Big Tony. "Yeah, he knows not to touch anyone – or he's out," said Tony.

"Well, we lost every delivery boy we had because of that man," replied the towel man. It seems that the linen service did all Pole's hotel laundry. They would find the linen truck abandoned in the middle of the route with no sign of the employees anywhere. They didn't even pick up their last check.

Old Pole

The employees were all young boys doing the deliveries, which was right down Pole's alley. Finally, they found the last group that quit and forced an explanation out of them. It seems that Pole (being unable to catch young men) would wait until they were in an enclosed place. A likely place would be the linen closet or the elevator. At this point Pole would throw himself on these young boys, absolutely terrifying them. The solution resolved itself, because thereafter all linens to Pole's hotel were thrown from a van traveling at no less than 40 m.p.h. in front of the hotel door.

Tony's gym was on the second floor on a crumbling brick building, located above a bail bondsman's place. Next door was a black nightclub called the Purple Onion. This nightclub catered to the lowest economic black population. The down-and-outs frequented the Onion. One could witness men dressed in suits made from velour stage curtains with matching hat. Or see a black midget drinking dredges out of old beer bottles in the dumpster. Always being the philosopher, Tony called his patrons over to the window one evening. "You boys, lookdown there on the sidewalk," he remarked.

There was a helpless black man so drunk he had to support himself by holding on to a parking meter. He had just staggered out of the Purple Onion.

Pole, seeing him in this condition was upon him in a flash. Unable to properly protect himself in this condition, the man was trying to kick Pole off of him. Pole was desperately clinging to one leg while the man was just as desperately clinging to the parking meter. "Hey man! Wad's wrong wid you? Lego my leg," shouted the drunk. Tony wisely advised his patrons with his sagely wisdom, "You see boys, Pole is like an old toothless African lion who can no longer catch his natural prey. Now he must exist on anything he can find like that helpless drunk there."

The football coach of the wealthy side of town came to Tony's Gym one day and was negotiating a contract for the entire team to train at Tony's place. This would be a tremendous sum of money for Tony, maybe more than a year's salary. Unfortunately for him, Animal-X and the perverted airline pilot were training just outside the office door. They were doing

169

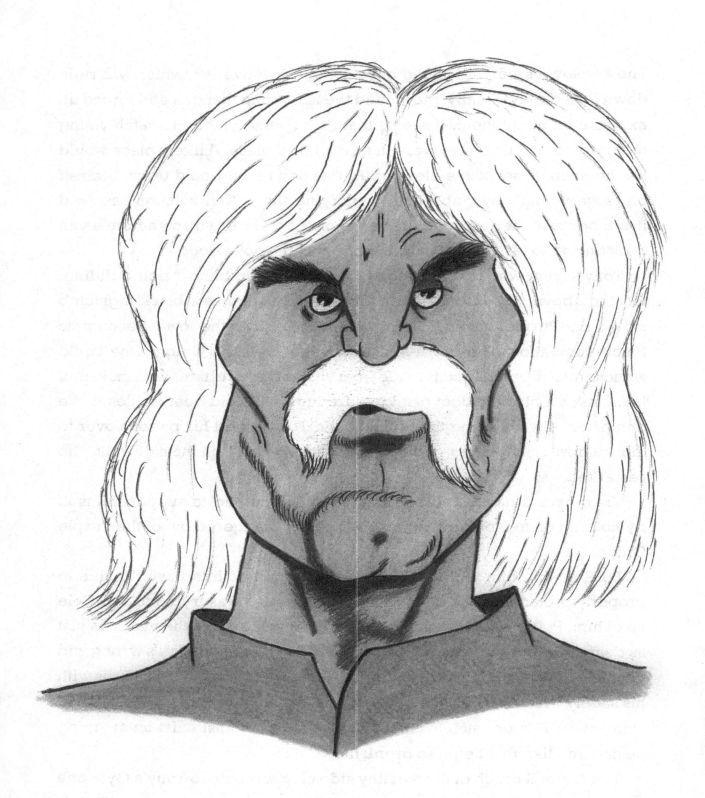

BIG TONY

"donkey calf raises". This exercise required the person working his calves to lean over a bench and step up on a block of wood to stretch out the muscles. The rider gets on the person's back near hip level providing extra weight while the calves are working up and down.

Never missing an opportunity to embarrass someone, the pilot began to squeal and moan, saying, "Stick it in deeper." The football coach just got up and without a word left the building. Tony was livid and Animal and the pilot were thrown out of the gym! "I shall cast thee down among the sodomites," yelled Tony, as he cursed them all the way out the door.

However, around six months later Tony cooled off and both guys were given a reprieve.

Big Tony enjoyed dining in one of the most exclusive restaurants located in the rich, old money part of the metroplex. After work hours he would visit the place on his way home.

The perverted airline pilot discovered this and would "pop-out" from behind the large granite pillars supporting the roof. He would pretend to be a flaming gay queen and shout at Big Tony. "Yoo-Hoo, Tonykins. That's my husband over there, the Big Man!" Tony would protest, which made the pilot even worse. "Now, Now," he would answer, "These people know how we are. You'll be alright after I get you home." It only took a few of these encounters for Tony to abandon the restaurant for all time.

If Tony ever used the airlines, the pilot would find out which flight he was returning on. He would fling himself on the man when he disembarked carrying his luggage, squealing and hugging Tony and acting gay. Tony would eventually develop a schism from all this. He would only travel from work to his home, and always by car.

Casanova got a job working in the bird section of a zoo in the Metroplex. There were many parrots on display for public viewing. The public came down an isle with the birds on perches on the opposite side of the counter. Behind the birds was a screen that the public could not see through, however, workers behind the screen could see the public clearly.

Casanova worked in that area frequently and began to "mimic" a parrot's voice. He became very adapt at sounding just like a real bird.

There were days that were slow because zoos are most active on weekends. On a slow day, Casanova was working behind the bird screen and an attractive woman came down the isle. Casanova gave out a bird whistle when she passed the parrot in front of him. The lady stopped and began to talk to the bird (some people actually think you can carry on a conversation with talking birds.) In the bird's voice, Casanova said, "squawk, whistle, you've got some nice tits there." "Do you think so," replied the woman. "How about a look," Casanova responded. She looked right and left to be sure no one was around, grabbed the bottom of her shirt and pulled it up to her face. Casanova got a great shot, however the bird was less impressed.

It was during this time frame that Casanova came into possession of a large quantity of male hormone for hoofstock. This was veterinary supply for things like zebras, horses and the like. He gave himself a huge injection of this and proceeded to a local whore house he knew about. In this establishment were different price ranges for different acts the people working there would perform. The most expensive price was to be able to have all the women there at one time. It was actually considered a joke, because no one had that kind of stamina. This is the thing Casanova most wanted. By the time he arrived the injection was starting to kick in. It was a night to remember. The man absolutely couldn't get enough. By the next morning all the women were crippled and limping around. Casanova took one woman's pair of glasses, sat it on the end of his dick and said, "Look around big boy and see if you missed anybody."

It is fortunate that the whorehouse was open because Casanova, in his condition, would have screwed a bush if he thought there was a bird in it.

In the summer months the amusement part of the zoo did an increased business and Casanova often found himself working there. His first costume was a space alien who was supposed to pat small children on the head as they entered the park. It was summer time and Casanova was sweating badly in the enclosed suit. The head piece had large insectoid eyes. Small perforated holes allowed the person in the suit to view the people without being viewed by them. When Casanova bent over to pat a kid on the head, all the sweat ran forward and began to spray out of the little eye holes. "Mama-Mama," said the kid, "the thing just spit on me!"

Casanova was given a less restrictive suit and was dressed in a rabbit costume. His job was to hug all the little kids. He quickly lost interest in hugging kids and moved to hugging good looking women. The horney rabbit was "complained on" and he was moved to a canoe ride.

The canoe ride put Casanova in an Indian outfit paddling customers around and artificial pond about two feet deep. Occasionally he got a boatload of people who didn't want to work, and all the paddling was left up to Casanova.

There was an overhanging tree heavily laden with water droplets from the morning sprinkler system. When Casanova got a bunch of lazy folk in the canoe he would paddle underneath the tree and jab an overhead limb with the paddle. He enjoyed getting these people wet.

One day he jabbed the limb and a six-foot rat snake fell out of the tree among the passengers. People actually walked on water getting away. Patrons fled in all directions as Casanova whacked the snake with the paddle and dumped it overboard. He could hear the commotion from the dock where most of his patrons escaped to. "Did you see that big mother fucker?" "Yes, and it almost bit me too!"

Casanova was fired that day, but later went across the river to his favorite place. This particular bar had a live band and a dance floor luminated from underneath. Fights frequently broke out in the place and spilled over on the dance floor. Dancing people simply moved over and continued to dance while the fighters flailed the living shit out of each other a few feet away. Occasionally some of the dancers would enter the fight, and the fighters would also stop and dance for a while with the extra women. The band continued playing all the while during this madness. Casanova was in heaven!

Casanova returned to the same saloon the next night with all his extended family and friends. They were all about to enter the place when a local preacher suddenly inserted himself between them and the door.

"Brothers," he shouted, "don't go in there. Why that place is filled with strong drink, games of chance and brazen women!" The preacher was subsequently trampled in a mad rush by the mob, bent on corrupting themselves.

Chapter 23

The 50's and early 60's was a time of non-interference and non-involvement. People did not openly disagree on many issues. There was clear cut right and wrong and good and bad. There wasn't a lot of gray areas. Dress codes at school were unknown. Most people were glad to have clothes that weren't patched. Some people's clothes were made at home and from feed sacks. When a child acted-out at school paddling was certain and swift. No questions asked!

People could burn their trash, build a barn, or paint their house without having to pay for "permits" as we do today. If a man beat his wife in public it was definitely noticed, certainly talked about, but there was no intervention. Police were rarely called and attorneys were not needed. People figured that the woman probably had it coming, or, if the man had gone too far, she would leave him. Others did not advise or get involved. Likewise, men were careful about what they said to each other. If your mouth over ran itself you were therefore accountable and at risk physically. There is an old saying, "Speak not with impudence, for a man may not choose to take it."

The actions of Catshit Looney would have never been tolerated today. Catshit would lurk in alleys and recessed store fronts waiting for smaller, weaker victims to pass by. Whereupon, he would spring upon them. Even if a person was armed, there was no time to get out a weapon. Once he got his hands on you, this sadist would squeeze, twist, and torment your body. He always stopped short of breaking bones, so if you complained about him you were viewed as a whiner.

Interestingly enough, no one would pull the bastard off of you even in a public place. People apparently considered it beyond their notice, or perhaps beneath their dignity.

This attitude did not extend to Animal-X or Axel Fender. Each one had little tolerance for what Catshit did to smaller people. The one occasion that Animal-X caught Catshit mauling someone was a memorable affair. For all of Catshit's speed and strength, he was like a child in the hands of Animal. When Animal was through beating on Catshit, his face looked like fifty cents worth of hamburger meat. After this incident Catshit was so much in fear of Animal, he would leave any area the man appeared at. Because Catshit lived in one of the abandoned stores downtown he was always in the most active areas of Briar Patch. This afforded him a constant supply of people to torment. If Axel Fender caught Catshit abusing someone, he would do to Catshit exactly what he had been doing to his victim. However, Catshit Looney was a slow learner.

Catshit felt that he could overpower Axel. One day at school he caught Axel getting off the bus. Before Axel saw him, Catshit unloaded his best shot. Being hit "unaware" is called being "sucker-punched." Axel just looked at Catshit, spat out some blood and meat, and said, "Is that all you've got? Hell, my old Daddy can hit harder than that!"

It wasn't long until Axel had Catshit down on the road, rubbing his face in the gravel. True-to-form, Axel continued to lecture Catshit during his chastisement. Because this was on school property, a large group of students gathered. Many of them were Catshit's former victims. All of them clambering for Axel to kill the son-of-a-bitch. Had it not been on school property, no interference would have occurred. Unfortunately school officials drug Axel off Catshit before the crowd was fully satisfied.

When Bookworm and his brother were quite small, their dad would play tricks on them. He liked to phone the house and get them on the phone. As soon as they were on the line, he would change his voice. He was quite gifted at this and would sound like an old crone.

"This is the wicked old witch, "he would say, "I'm coming over to your house and eat you little boys." After this statement he would cackle insanely. At this point he would hand the phone to his fellow workers who could hear the kids on the other end on the phone running and screaming. Bookworm was convinced that these calls were coming from the towns old hag, Ruff Briar. It never occurred to him that Ruff had no phone nor the money to use a pay phone. Consequently, anytime his grandmother let Ruff in the house, Bookworm was all "assholes and elbows" in an attempt to escape.

Fox, of the Creature clan, continued to attempt to civilize the clan. He was constantly admonishing Wolf about his eating habits. "Wolf", he would

176

say, "Don't let those flies crawl on your food. Flies crawling on food is bad." Wolf would just shrug and say, "But Fox, they eat so little."

Like the rest of the Briar Patch crowd, B.O. Sharp tried his hand at the sport of weight lifting. He never went to the metroplex. Animal-X had a home gym in which he was more comfortable. Despite B.O.'s lack of coordination, he was quite gifted in brute power. He came close to lifting some world records. B.O. figured that if he could gain thirty additional pounds, he would be able to set new power lifting records. Not a tall man, and already weighing approximately 300 pounds, there wasn't room to gain another 30 pounds. B.O. was so thick that his head sat directly on his shoulders. His neck had somehow disappeared in the bulking process of weight lifting There was no way he could button a collar or wear a tie. His fingers, although short, were as huge as bananas. While Animal-X could bend a horseshoe, B.O. could sometimes break one in two pieces.

B.O. began to expand his lunch volume in order to gain the needed weight. He would carry his lunch to work in a suitcase. The suitcase would have two loaves of bread made into sandwiches and a half-gallon of milk on ice. All of these attempts to gain weight failed. It seems that B.O. had already saturated his frame for weight. Carrying this much body weight created an enormous amount of body heat. B.O. could sweat while standing outside in a snowdrift. He slept in an air-conditioned room during winter with only a sheet for cover.

Desperate to gain the necessary thirty pounds, he asked Animal-X what he should do. Animal was reluctant to advise about anything, considering B. O.'s situation. "B.O.", he said, "You can't carry 30 more pounds. You'll have a heart attack and die!" Hell, you already look like you're in your third tri-mester. B.O. kept after him until Animal finally relented. He told him about a product carried by a certain grocery store in the pharmacy section. However, you don't need a prescription to buy it. The product is "high-octane carbohydrates" that you mix with milk. It is designed for people fresh out of starvation and is used for anorexia and similar problems. "It'll put weight on a fence post." "Well, I've got to get some of that," replied B.O.

Briar Patch didn't have a store sophisticated enough for this product, so B.O. had to travel to a larger near-by town. He asked the local pharmacist, "I want to buy some Susta-butt." The pharmacist took one look at B.O. (who looked like a rolling man-hole cover) and said, "Is this for you?" "Yeah, it's for me," replied B.O. "Do you know what this stuff is for?" inquired the man. "Yeah, I need to gain 30 pounds," B.O. remarked. "Well", asked the pharmacist, "Did your doctor prescribe this?" "What", said B.O., "Do you think my doctor's crazy?"

At this point the pharmacist began to laugh uncontrollably. He called all the other store employees over to see B.O. and his unusual request. Everyone was amused at B.O.'s expense. So B.O. left the store without his Susta-butt. Not to be denied, he purchased it at another store, where he lied about its use. Even this product failed to put on any more weight on B.O. and his doctor made him lose weight due to his increased blood pressure.

Axel Fender decided to try his hand at police work. He applied at a nearby larger town and was accepted. During his first year on the force he was assigned a college intern who was interested in a career in criminal justice. They rode together in the squad car almost every day. During a routine day they received a (code-ten) dispatch, which means anyone nearby should go to the address of an outgoing offense.

Upon arrival at the address they discovered they were in the section of town known as, "Little Mexico". Apparently a wino had crawled up under a house and died there. No one seemed to notice any smell because this house had no plumbing. In one corner of the living room a large hole had been chopped into the floor. This hole was the household bathroom facility. The dead wino was discovered when a dog dragged the body out from its resting place. The entire premises smelled highly putrid. Axel told the intern, "We've got to get away from this mess!"

He informed the Hispanic family that they must make an additional phone call to summon another squad to the scene. This confused them and they said, "But you are the police!" "Yes," replied Axel, "That's true, but for this work you need to call the cops!" "Oh," said the complainant, "The cops, of course. We will call right away." Axel and the intern got away

with this indiscretion and the intern changed his major from police work to business.

For all Dr. Feelgood's knowledge, he knew very little in certain areas. He continued to drink with Casanova and seek his advice about women. Casanova was the very last person from whom anyone should seek counseling. Feelgood would complain that his wife would withhold sex for the smallest infraction, or even for imagined transgressions. "What you've got on your hands," said Casanova, "is a genuine pussy terrorist! No pussy for you tonight! Your only recourse is to masturbate frequently, so that when she pulls this stunt you can say, "Thank God, I couldn't possibly have performed one more time." This disarms a pussy terrorist, because that's all she's got!" Casanova threw in some lyrics at this point that had the doctor completely mesmerized: "A pussy is a marvelous thing beyond compare; smells like a rotten potato and looks like the ass of a bear!"

Later in the evening the good doctor and Casanova quit beer and moved on to hard liquor. This got them to where they were headed a lot faster than beer would have. Unfortunately Feelgood, who was not accustomed to strong drink, passed out. Casanova was drunk enough to believe that the doctor had had a stroke. Casanova summoned an ambulance and Feelgood was admitted to "Our Lady of Pain and Suffering Hospital". Feelgood's entire extended family was alerted and some arrived in various stages of disrobement, curlers in the hair, etc. All were alarmed about his condition.

The head nurse informed them all that he was just drunk, which angered some of them for highly undue inconvenience. His wife refused to take him home and said, "Just leave him here." The next morning Feelgood awoke in a strange place. Looking around, he didn't know where he was, or how he had gotten there. He did notice the name of the hospital on his bed sheets. The embarrassed doctor got dressed, checked himself out, and called a taxi. Now the doctor had a hospital and ambulance bill, in addition to having to face the wrath of his wife.

Mrs. Feelgood said, "So, you got drunk with your friend, Old King Cole, (which is what she called Casanova). When you passed out he had you put in the hospital. It serves you right for embarrassing everyone. I hope he does this to you every time you two get drunk." Feelgood's drinking was drastically reduced thereafter.

Casanova continued to educate the doctor in "street smarts", which basically amounted to "attempted corruption". "When I run low on money," said Casanova, "I just 'roll some queers'". "What's that?" asked Feelgood. "You just beat them up and rob them," explained Casanova. "How do you know who to roll?" asked the doctor. "Well," said Casanova, "It's a known fact that all queers wear green on Thursday. These people are fair game! Anyone who forgets and wears green on that day is expendable. It does become problematic if St. Patrick's Day falls on a Thursday. However, Thursday is handy because I need money the next day for the weekend." Be careful though, because some queers are fast and strong. They might "throw you and blow you" before you can "roll um and hold um."

"Likewise," continued Casanova, 'Whores wear red on Mondays. Some of them play (hard-to-get), but for five dollars will sometimes invite you back to their place for a sexual experience with a goat." Casanova went on to indoctrinate Feelgood with his poetic "pearls of wisdom."

A girl with eyes of blue will never be true to you.
A girl with eyes of green is sly and vicious and mean.
A girl with eyes of brown will cheat on you and run around.
A girl with eyes of black will stick a dagger in your back.
A girl with eyes of gray will lie to you every day.
And remember, a one-eyed girl is half blind.

Casanova also supplied this bit of useful information:
The cabin boy, the cabin boy, that sneaky little nipper, put broken glass up his ass and circumcised the skipper.

Casanova and Animal-X were briefly hired at an exotic animal park. Their employment was brief because of Casanova's pranks and capers. This particular park was an educational walk through affair with a guide.

Casanova was the guide, and groups numbered about a dozen people per trip. Because this park was not large they employed a few "gimmicks" to encourage patronage. Their best trick was to advertise the only semi-captive sasquatch to be seen anywhere. This creature was reported to be "at-large" on the zoo grounds. The actual creature was Animal-X, who because of his size, got to wear the sasquatch suit. His job was to run ahead of the group and peep out at them from incomplete hiding. Buildings, bushes, etc., were his choices of concealment. His size, behavior, and suit quality was apparently quite convincing and many people were convinced that they were seeing the real thing.

Casanova asked Animal to do something at the end of the tour to enhance his performance. He told Animal that upon his signal, to come charging toward the group and break off the run just before closure. What he failed to tell Animal was what he planned to tell the group. All went well that day until Casanova signaled Animal to charge the group. "Oh my God," shouted Casanova, "If he catches you, he'll fuck you. Everyone run for your life." Needless to say, their tenure at this job was a very brief one.

After Axel lost his sidekick, the intern, he continued to do police work. One day he stopped a man from Louisiana. The gentleman obviously had a Cajun name of French ancestry. His license listed his last name as "Pussi". "The reason I stopped you Mr. Pussy is because your tail lights are out," said Axel. The man protested and said, "That's pronounced Pa-say." "I'm sorry, Mr. Pussy, I can't speak French. You're going to have to fix that taillight Mr. Pussy." Axel continued to address him as Mr. Pussy for the duration of their contact.

Soon after that incident Axel discovered, even though he could not speak French, he could speak Vietnamese. It seems that a car full of Vietnamese people had slipped off the road and were stuck in a muddy ditch. "Aahhha", said Axel, "you stucky-stucky." Since the victims talked the same way, no offense was taken.

One night Animal-X was in a club across the river when a young couple (barely twenty-one years old) came in and sat at a nearby table. Now these two were just kids in comparison to many of the seasoned ruffians who

182

**EYES
WIGGLESWORTH**

frequented the place. Three of those uncouth troublemakers decided they wanted the young lady and asked her to dance. She politely refused! Soon all three of them were at the table requesting a dance quite insistently. It would merely be a question of moments before they broke the little guy in pieces and took his woman.

Animal wouldn't tolerate such behavior in his presence. Suddenly he appeared in the midst of these three and said, "I want to dance with all three of you outside right now!" After going outside Animal took on all three of them at the same time. An ambulance was promptly summoned to the scene as all three required medical attention. None could leave under his own power. The kid Animal had saved thanked him and said, "I couldn't have done that." "I know," replied Animal, "but its ok. I could, and besides, it was needed."

Another Briar Patch character named Eyes Wigglesworth could generally be found at gatherings. Eyes sees all, knows all, and tells all! Basically the man was a con artist, instigator and information whore. His talents were congenial and most people weren't even aware of what he was up to. He conned family members into doing his homework for his first eight school years. This failed to work in high school so he spent four years in the ninth grade and quit when he was not socially promoted. He seemed to know in detail what everyone in town owned and made it his business to notice everything. He loved to start trouble between people, then step aside and watch the fun. He never used his own car because he flattered, entertained, and conned his way everywhere as a passenger.

Animal-X decided to fix up the car he had by putting a full-race camshaft in it. Animal knew his mechanical ability was limited and was looking for affordable, professional assistance. Bandit, was of course, out-of-the-question. Eyes learned of this and raved long and loud about an expert mechanic he knew that would be willing to perform this task for free.

There was an abandoned garage near the railroad that was available for use. On the day of the "anointing," many hot rod enthusiasts were on hand. There was a festive air when "Shade-tree Charlie" arrived at the garage with his toolbox.

Meanwhile, during the dismantling of the motor, Eyes had the opportunity to apply his talents as an opportunist and manipulator. So, as a sideshow event, he persuaded four or five of the stronger guys to pull the pants off of Jimmy the Louse, who was there and had annoyed him. Once the pants were off, Eyes took a stick and smeared a large glob of grease on Louse's privates from the grease bucket. Eyes would have been powerless to promote this act without his powers of persuasion.

As for the car, the great moment arrived when the new camshaft was put in place. The motor was re-assembled and everyone was awaiting the magic moment of ignition. Animal got in the car and attempted to start it up. Unfortunately "Shade-tree Charlie" wasn't quite as good as Eyes had claimed. The new cam wasn't put in properly and promptly bent every push rod in the motor, in addition to causing other damage. Everyone simply shied away and left Animal alone with his decimated motor. He even had to walk home. Animal had his car towed to another town for repair. He received much verbal abuse from his parents and also from the "real mechanic" who had to salvage this mess.

Comments from the mechanic were, "Who's been fucking with this distributor?" Animal answered, "Charlie has, does that information help you at all?" Eyes lost a lot of credibility over the incident and Animal never again took his advice. After all, it wasn't Eyes who had to pay for the damage.

Chapter 24

Billy Bob McKnob brought home an old "Bar-Fly" one evening. Both of them had been drinking heavily and they got into a heated argument. Being short tempered, McKnob drew his pistol, pointed it at her crotch and pulled the trigger. Unable to undo the damage, he decided to call Dr. Feelgood. "Feelgood," he slurred, "I just shot a woman in the snatch! What should I do now?" The doctor assumed that this was a prank, so he said, "that's a hard act to follow. Why don't you just set your ass on fire and fart The Eyes of Texas!" Eventually McKnob convinced the doctor that this was a serious matter. Feelgood summoned an ambulance to McKnob's residence and instructed him to meet him at the next town's police station. Things would look better, according to the doctor, if McKnob turned himself in and said it was an accident. Arriving at the police station the two attempted to explain the situation. Unfortunately the whole station was in a high state of agitation and near panic. Apparently this town never got much action or crimes of a serious nature.

"We don't have time for you right now," said the officer, "A report just came in that a mad carnal shootist is at large and we're trying to find him."

After a good deal of chasing the officers around the building, the situation was finally explained to them. Sanity was restored and McKnob went through lengthy discomfort until the matter was eventually settled. "You know," remarked McKnob, "That Bobbitt woman can cut her husbands dick off, and everyone laughs about it, but you just try shooting a woman's snatch and all hell breaks loose."

Another similar incident happened soon after Animal X returned from Viet Nam and discovered Bunny was being unfaithful to him. In the early stages of this discovery, Animal became completely irrational. The man was usually level headed and sensible in most matters. Only where bunny was concerned did he go completely "haywire."

Animal began to stalk Bunny and one day showed up outside her place of work with a loaded shotgun. Bunny was just arriving at the location in her car when Animal stuck the gun in the car window and said, "If I can't have

187

you, no one is going to have you!" No one will ever know if he was bluffing or not because Bunny quickly rolled up the window, which bumped the shotgun and caused it to discharge.

At this point, Animal realized things had gotten out of control. He panicked and drove straight to Axel Fenders house.

Axel was taking his morning shower when suddenly the shower door was jerked open and he and Animal just stood there looking at each other, speechless. (Reminiscent of the movie "Psycho.") "What the hell are you doing?" shouted Axel. "I just shot my wife," said Animal. "Get the hell out of here while I get dressed," replied Axel. He quickly got dry and threw on some clothes, only to discover that Animal had vanished. While wondering where he had gone, Axel heard someone knocking on his door. Arriving at the door, he discovered Animal outside. Apparently Animal was stressed out and wanted to start over from scratch.

"Is Bunny dead?" asked Axel. "I don't know, it was an accident. I just drove straight over here," said Animal. "You dumb son-of-a-bitch, what in the hell were you thinking," shouted Axel. Then he began to think, this guy has already shot one person this morning, I had better back off of him or I just might be next! "We should calm down and work this out," said Axel. Take your car down the road, away from my house. I'll call in at work and pick you up in case they're looking for your car.

Axel had just been hired as an assistant coach at a nearby town and didn't need this kind of attention at his new job. "I'll be a couple of hours late today," he told the principal. "Can you cover for me for awhile?" "What's the problem?" asked his boss. "It's a personal problem and I promise it won't happen ever again," said Axel.

As Axel and Animal pulled on to the highway, the ambulance transporting Bunny was also pulling on to the same road. It was strange, as both men watched the paramedics working on Bunny through the back glass windows. They followed and watched until the ambulance turned right for the hospital and they turned left for the police department. Arriving at the police station, they approached the front desk. "Have a seat, "the receptionist said, "We have an emergency right now!" So, Axel and Animal sat a while and listened to the elevator music. Meanwhile, the police station is acting like an ant nest someone kicked over. Axel again tried to approach the receptionist and was told quiet firmly to remain seated, as this was not a good time to be bothering them. They continued to listen to the elevator music and could hear the physical description of Animal being broadcast all over the department. Height, weight, hair and eye color, clothes, etc. and the man is right here in plain sight. Finally Axel again approached the receptionist and said, "Are you looking for someone who just shot his wife?" "Yes, how did you know?" replied the receptionist. "Because, I've been trying to tell you.........he's right over here," answered Axel.

They handcuffed Animal and finger printed him. Axel was asked if he would be a witness, which he declined, as he was very late for work. "I only gave him a ride, that's all," said Axel.

As it turned out, Bunny was only shot in one leg and it was not serious. Animal said it was an accident, so no serious charges were brought against him.

After Axel quit working for the police department many years later, he began to do secret, undercover work for them. It seems that occasionally there is a crook so successful that the police can never catch him. Axel was used in this capacity when such emergencies arose. The routine was one of fear and intimidation, sort of fighting fire with fire.

Axel would wear a ski mask and break into the perpetrators house. If he could not just walk in, he would kick open the door and shout, "Candy gram for Mr. Mongel." This usually gave people reason to hesitate, at which time Axel would shoot tranquilizer darts into everyone in the house. Sometimes Axel would shout other "one liners" for variety. On one occasion he burst in the door yelling, "Did you hear about the two queer judges that tried each other?" As soon as the criminal would come around to consciousness, Axel would council him! "You've been doing illegal things," he would say. "If they don't stop, the next time you see me will be much, much worse." He would then re-tranquilize the subject with another dart. On the perpetrator's second awakening, he would discover Axel had gone. This system, although unorthodox, was extremely successful. After all, Axel could have done anything he wanted while his victim was unconscious.

Crash had recently gotten a job in a store that was basically dry goods but carried all manner of supplies. One day the cashier was checking out a customer when she came to an item with no price tag on it. Since Crash was stocking shelves, she could quickly find the items price for her. The cashier got on the intercom system by her station and announced all over the store, "What price is a box of Tampax?" Crash mistakenly thought she asked for the price of a box of thumbtacks. So naturally she intercomed back, all over the store..........."The ones you push in with your thumb are $1.25 a box, but the ones you have to beat in with a hammer are $1.50 a box." Business just got better!

One of Bookworm's jobs at home was to bring in the cows every evening from pasture to the barn. He usually rode their old horse, "Ajax" for this task. Ajax was rather large and Bookworm had to climb the corral fence in order to mount up. During summer months, there was no need for a saddle; in fact, bookworm was usually barefoot and very informally attired.

While in the process of getting the cattle to the barn, bookworm had an urgent need to urinate. He knew if he dismounted for this activity, there was no way he could re-mount without the corral fence. He solved this problem by standing up on the horses hips and urinating off the side. This redistributing of his weight caused Ajax to step sideways and walk around a bit. Unfortunately this moving about directed the stream of urine right into an electric fence! Bookworm was "lit-up" like a Christmas tree but worst of all Ajax got shocked too, because bookworm was standing on him. Ajax shot out from under bookworm who was left standing six feet in mid-air with his dick in his hand. So, never piss off a horse.

After Boscoe and Ruff moved from Briar Patch they began to go to many public places with their newly acquired income. The first place they frequented was dinner playhouses and theaters in the metroplex. They were at their first play one evening that featured a murder mystery or, "who-done-it" as they are commonly known. During the live performance both Boscoe and Ruff were mesmerized by the performance. They became

190

so caught up in the play that both of them forgot that it wasn't real. Close to the end of the performance, some stage characters shot the villain who collapsed on stage. Both Ruff and Boscoe jumped to their feet, slapping their knees and shouting, "They shot that son-of-a-bitch; they shot that son-of-a-bitch!" All the patrons of the audience stared at them, wondering if this was a part of the show. The actors were stunned, and even the "shot villain" revived to see what the disturbance was all about. Boscoe and Ruff continued to hop about shouting obscenities and celebrating the villain's demise. It is interesting to note that no one knows what to do in a situation like this!

It was during this time period that fried pies first appeared in stores. The pies were folded over into a half-circle shape, with apricot filling. Fox and Wolf of the Creature clan had some proceeds from their rat catching business and decided to buy a couple of these good smelling things. While eating them, Fox commented, "This is good, how do you like yours?" Wolf replied, "It's good, but Wolf's pie is kind of tough." At this point, Fox noticed that Wolf was eating the pie, cardboard and all. He suggested, "I think I know what's wrong with yours."

B. O. Sharp had recently won a bet that he could lose one hundred pounds in a one month time period. This was an amazing act in itself; however, it was more surprising that he entered a power lifting contest at this depleted body weight. B. O. had dropped from two hundred eighty-five pounds to one hundred eighty pounds. No one at the contest recognized him. None of his friends spoke to him at all. When he weighed in, the official (who had known him for years) asked, "Name!" B. O. gave his name and was laughed at. "No," he said, "It's really me. I'm in here!" Poor B. O. was definitely washed-out, wrung-out and dried-out! In this depleted condition he was very weak.

Now, it just-so-happened that one of the prominent lifters wives had decided to enter the contest. This was a "first," as power lifting at that time was considered a man's sport. The lady had gained a lot of weight for the event, trained hard, and was feeling strong. Unfortunately she and B. O. were in the same weight class.

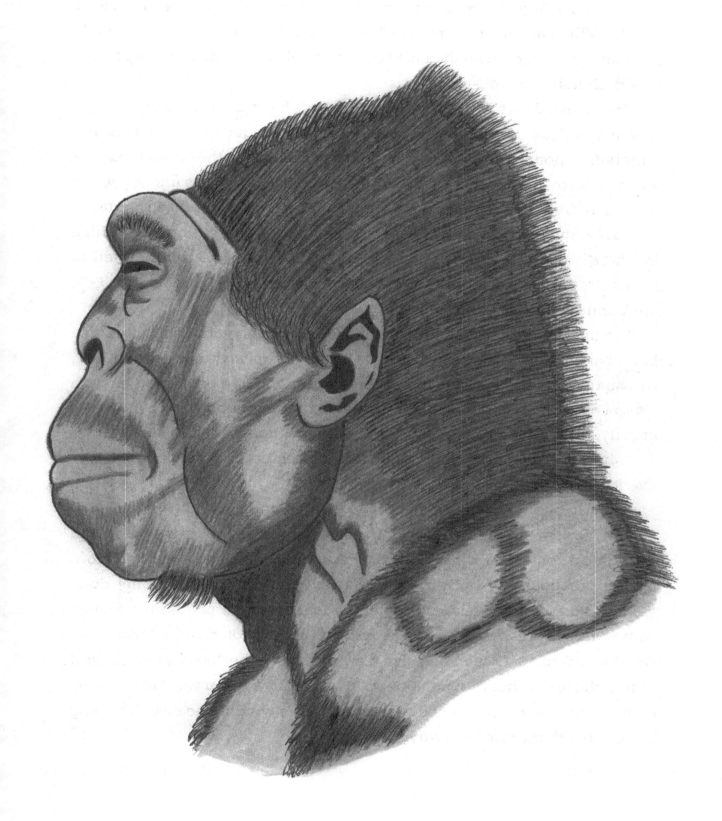

It is interesting to note, that when a man gains weight, it is referred to as "bulk." When a woman gains weight it is regarded as "fat." This probably has something to do with the muscle mass involved. So, B. O.'s competition was definitely "bulked-up."

They started out with the "bench press." Each contestant gets three attempts and the heaviest one is counted. B. O. managed to get two hundred twenty-five pounds in his wrenched condition. Before the weight loss, he was at approximately five hundred pounds in this lift. It was enough to put him out in front as women are not known for their upper body strength.

Next came the "full-squat." The lady had massive thighs and ass, which is where most of the body's power lies. B. O.'s legs had deteriorated to sticks and his ass looked like two walnuts in a sock. Needless to say, B. O. fell behind badly in this competition.

The final lift is the "dead lift," which is mostly using your back with some leg involvement. This was not a lift B. O. had vigorously trained for. In fact, he usually only did it at the actual contest, and then he only lifted enough weight as was needed to win. By the time this lift rolled around, B. O. was usually so far ahead that he could win easily without exerting himself.

"My God," thought B. O., I'm about to be beaten by a woman! I'll never live it down!"

Because she was so far ahead, B. O. had to strain his "guts out" just to tie her. Now, in the case of a tie, both contestants must be re-weighted and the lightest contestant wins. That is because the lightest person lifted more weight per pound of body weight. However, re-weighting is only done naked and the lady's husband objected loudly to this act. So the female contestant was re-weighted by the wife of the promoter and all was well. As it turned out, B. O. won because the woman was the "heavier man," as it is called. He was heard commenting to her, "Lady, if you want to compete against me again............you'd better gain some weight because I'm going back to two-hundred eighty-five pounds!"

Chapter 25

Ruff and her new husband Boscoe were traveling in his car, a true act of faith when he was at the wheel! It was not uncommon for Boscoe to clean out bar ditches on both sides of the road while driving his vehicle. Sometimes this was in an attempt to run over varmints (his favorite pastime), but often it was just his inability to see the road.

Ruff began to complain, "Damn you Boscoe, pull this thing over somewhere! I need to shit!"

Boscoe responded with "Can't you hold it until we get home?"

"No, you son-of-a-bitch! I got to go now!"

As Boscoe felt Ruff was being very unreasonable, he said "To hell with that! Just crap in a jug!"

Ruff responded by lowering the car window, sticking out her ass and "letting go".

Now it just so happened that Firewater Barstool and Billy Bob McKnob were walking down this same road. Both men were already drunk, even though it was the middle of the day.

McKnob said, "Damn it, Barstool, did you see that guy in the car that just went by? The bastard spit tobacco juice all over us!"

"Hell," said Barstool, "that's nothing! Did you notice the size of those jaws of his?"

Later that evening the two drunks retired to an alley in town, where they drank several bottles of cheap cooking wine. They would lay among the garbage cans, swilling the worst "rot-gut" available and pretend to be connoisseurs of the most sensitive and refined palate.

McKnob would comment, "Mine's a fine, dry, high altitude, white vintage with a light bouquet, what's yours?"

Barstool would reply with "Mine's a bold, red burgundy, with only a hint of pretentiousness."

Bookworm sometimes hung around McKnob, but it was always a risky business. McKnob would sit under a shade tree and put away an entire case of beer without getting up to urinate. Bookworm was very impressed with this accomplishment – until he learned that the man had a hose hooked to his dick! The hose traveled down one pants leg and emptied on the ground. "I always wondered why no grass grew under that tree," commented the Worm.

One day McKnob sold Bookworm some "smart pills".

"Damn," said Bookworm, "this tastes like rabbit shit!"

"See there," said McKnob, "you're getting smarter already."

Bookworm seemed to be born with the mind and thoughts of an adult. He didn't seek the company of children his age, considering them immature.

Bookworm never truly trusted adults. It all started when he was a small child and he realized his parents were lying to him. At three years old, his tonsils were removed and his parents told him it wouldn't hurt. He knew that wasn't so.

Next, they lied about Santa Clause. His mother would say, "You won't get anything for Christmas if you're bad, because Santa knows everything you do." By this time, Bookworm was five, and by his reckoning, quite sophisticated. "Bullshit!" said the boy, "That fat bastard doesn't know what I'm doing, if he exists at all!"

Bookworm's mom never knew quite how to deal with this. She was always underestimating him. Thinking quickly, she said, "You see all the little birds in the trees and the bushes? They watch you all the time – and they fly to the North Pole to tell Santa what you are doing."

"My god," thought Bookworm, " those damn, lying birds are everywhere – and always watching, too."

The next big lie was when his mother attempted to disguise his medicine by putting it in a Coke bottle and coloring the liquid red. Although red was Bookworm's favorite color, he knew Cokes weren't red. "I'm not drinking that shit!" he said.

His mother still hadn't given up on the Santa "gig". One Christmas Mr. Smith, a fat neighbor, dressed up like Santa for the downtown parade. Bookworm's mom had persuaded the man to stop by her house before he went home to take the costume off.

The man came in their house and did the "Ho-ho-ho" thing. Then he asked Bookworm, "Have you been a good boy this year?"

"Don't you know?", asked Bookworm. "You've got those lying birds running their mouths about me!"

Santa didn't quite know what to make of this, and quickly departed. After he was gone, Bookworm told his mom, "I think that was our neighbor, Mr. Smith." The woman was completely taken a-back. The boy was obviously beyond his years of five.

The next big lie was his mother telling him he would like school. Bookworm already knew he didn't want anything to do with leaving home. He saw school as a very negative prospect. "I'm smart enough," argued the Worm. "I don't need to go to that school."

However, as soon as he turned six years old, his mother drove him to that schoolhouse. "Let's get out and go in so we can see what they're doing," said his mother. "If you want to know what they're doing so damned bad," responded the Worm, "you go in and find out. Then you can come back and tell me."

At this point, Bookworm was forcefully hauled into the building. The place was full of abandoned kids his own age – and some were crying, too! He kept his eyes on his mom. "That bitch is planning on leaving me here forever," he thought.

Sure enough, she made her break during recess. The Worm looked over to see their pickup leaving. Quick as a flash, he darted through a hole in the fence. "That fat teacher can't catch *me*," he thought. However, he could hear her screaming in the background. Looking back, he could see all the other kids staring, bug-eyed and open-mouthed.

Bookworm knew how to get home, taking short-cuts through yards and fields, so he arrived at home about the same time mom's truck did. She was not pleased and took a belt to him. He was returned to school and made to stay.

However, at three-thirty, the authority figures and teachers became either bored or lax, because everyone escaped and ran home.

For his entire first year of school, Bookworm believed his parents were trying to get rid of him on a daily basis. He also believed the students escaped every day. Adults were all a pack of liars and not to be trusted.

People forced you to do things you didn't want to do because they were bigger than you. They were strong enough to impose their will on you and you had nothing to say about it. You were forced to attend school, church, and Vacation Bible School. Bookworm despised all three of these. He noticed that his father didn't have to go to any of these places. He reasoned the man was bigger and stronger than the woman, who was forcing a small boy to comply. The only answer he could see was to get big and strong enough to do what he wanted to do instead of what he was made to do. Unfortunately, Bookworm suffered from poor health – and by the ninth grade, he was still the smallest person in his class. He entered high school at just five feet and one half inches tall, weighing only one hundred five pounds. Everyone bullied him and he became a social recluse.

In spite of all of this, the boy still got into mischief. He just tended to do it alone instead of with other people. Once, during his junior high school years, he went out to his grandmother's car to get his swimsuit out of the back seat. One of the windows was down and a stray cat was lying on his suit inside the car. Then he noticed that cat hairs were all over the suit. Even the animals seemed to have no respect for him! This final indignity caused him to quickly roll up the window of the car, trapping the animal inside and scaring the begeebers out of it. The cat was wild anyway – and it tore around the car interior looking for a place to get out. Every window it came to found Bookworm on the other side of the glass yelling. The cat flew from dashboard to package tray, over the seats, under the seats, and all around the sides. Unfortunately, it peed on everything it touched during the process.

Bookworm's grandmother, who owned the car, was watching this spectacle unfold. Luckily for him, she saw the humor in it. Bookworm's dad was bent on administering another beating to the boy for it, but the grandmother persuaded him not to, because she had enjoyed watching the whole thing.

When Bookworm entered college, he began socializing with a co-ed from a distant town. After the first semester, the girl had to drop out of school because she was pregnant. However, Bookworm had never touched her sexually. He was relating this sad story to Casanova Goodbody one day. Far from being the world's most sensitive person, Casanova responded with, "Well, Bookworm, I think somebody's been fuckin' your girlfriend!"

About this time, many of the neighbors that lived around Bookworm's parents were beginning to die of old age. (There is no leading cause of death for people in excess of one hundred years old.) Since the neighbors' children had long since married and left to create homes of their own, the third generation began to move into these houses. Interestingly enough, all of them were girls with illegitimate babies and no husbands.

These girls in question were so dysfunctional that no man could live with them. In short, their parents had failed as parents. That end of town became a dumping area for people's indiscretions. Bookworm's dad, who was appalled at all this, unofficially re-named their road "East Bastard Street".

It was during this time that Bookworm's dad made the mistake of renting some of his property to some very obese people. Upon moving in, they promptly destroyed all of his furniture with their tonnage. Couches and chairs were so mauled by these people that they were suddenly developing broken legs on a regular basis – and Bookworm's dad had to replace them frequently. The mattresses broke down in record time, too. Bookworm's dad remarked, "Can you imagine a rhino stomping on this bed? That's what happens when a couple of these four-hundred-pounders start screwing on it!"

The final straw was an incident involving a couple of these behemoths and a balcony. It seems a mother and her son went out on a second story balcony. Their combined weight totaled approximately one thousand pounds. At this load limit, the balcony simply tore loose from the building. Both mother and son broke their legs in the incident. Now totally disillusioned with humanity, Bookworm's dad just sold the property.

Bookworm and his dad had a very unusual relationship. Bookworm's mother admitted she couldn't handle the boy. He was strong-willed and usually one step ahead of her.

The dad said, "He gets it from my side of the family. I know how to deal with it!" He further confessed that his mother had a brother that had to be tied up during the daytime hours. It seems the brother tended to run away. It was impossible for them to do their work *and* watch him at the same time. Since this took place in West Texas during the eighteen hundreds, if he had run away, it was likely he would have been killed by Indians.

Bookworm's dad was short tempered and could turn violent in an instant. On those occasions when he "went off", he would beat Bookworm severely. Neighbors could hear these beatings from over a block away. The man would grab a board, a garden hose, or anything else he could lay his hands on with which to administer punishment. If he could control himself long enough to get the boy in the house, his favorite tool was a razor strap. It seemed just beating Bookworm wasn't enough; he would curse the boy while he laid it on. His favorite passage was, "Damn your soul!"

Bookworm had developed the habit of calling his dad a son-of-a-bitch at the conclusion of these encounters, which then caused the process to be repeated. This type of man was never really suited to raise children. However, like most people today, they did it anyway! This violence continued until Bookworm was seventeen years old. The man was lucky Bookworm wasn't born with a body like Animal-X or B.O. Sharp. If *that* had been the case, the boy just might have turned on him.

At seventeen years of age, Bookworm noticed the beatings suddenly stopped. It might have been that Bookworm was now a normal-sized person and the father was starting to be ashamed of himself. The anger was still there, only now it was somewhat controlled.

This bizarre upbringing caused Bookworm to hate and fear the man – but he also loved him, too! In later years, Bookworm reasoned that perhaps his father's behavior was justified to keep him in line. There was no way to truly know.

This destructive pattern was broken because Bookworm never married or had children. Statistics show that someone raised in this manner feels it is normal and will likely repeat the process. We know this is true in Casanova Goodbody's family history.

Chapter 26

Dr. Feelgood had a friend who was a acting judge in a neighboring county. When the judge was in town, they would have lunch together. As a visiting judge, he saw a lot of stimulating cases.

He remarked to Feelgood one day, "You know, there are a lot of exciting cases in your county. Why, you have rape, murder, burglary, armed robbery, narcotics, and a variety of other crimes. In my county, we only seem to have crimes of incest – and the worst thing about this problem is that the subjects don't seem to believe there is anything wrong with it!"

Feelgood was having an office cookout during the early evening hours for the patients and staff. During this time of the year mosquitoes were very bad. The doctor asked Crash to go to the store for some bug spray because, as he commented, " These bugs are going to carry us off!".

Feelgood just assumed that Crash knew enough to buy "Off!" or some similar brand of mosquito repellent. As usual, he was wrong. She returned with Raid Roach and Ant Killer. Apparently, "bugs" was a broad terminology to Crash.

During the party, Crash saw a mouse eating a roach under a yard light. This fascinated her and she mentioned it to Feelgood.

"What did you think mice ate?" replied the doctor.

"Why, I thought all mice ate was cheese," said Crash.

Well, you know, mice have been around long before people learned how to make cheese. What about the mice who don't have a house of cheese-eating people to live with? Do you think they all just hang around free government cheese programs?

Feelgood was certain that whomever Crash married was going to have his hands full and his work cut out for him.

The nearest metroplex had a major river meandering through the middle of the city. During the 1950's and the 1960's, sewage was routinely dumped into this particular river – and you could smell it for miles. The southeast end of town was particularly bad because the river flowed in that direction. There was a vast flood plain on both sides that was considered "No Man's Land". Houses were only built within a certain distance of this area of silt and mud, as it was considered unsafe to venture too close. Over the decades, as the city grew and expanded, this "No Man's Land" became the nation's largest illegal dump. Mountains of refuse were created, which spanned acres and acres of old furniture, tires, and trash of all sorts. These "mountains" of debris reached heights of forty feet or more. All efforts to halt this practice failed. Trucks just ran to new openings when old ones were sealed off. The illegal dumping now continued day and night without pause. It seems once a practice of this nature begins, it's almost impossible to stop it.

This nasty eyesore that was home to old car bodies, broken down furniture, and virtually any other repulsive thing you could imagine by day, was also home to many unseen, nocturnal creatures. There were untold numbers of feral cats, dogs, opossums, coons, and snakes who called this vast dumping ground home! Innumerable amounts of mice and rats abounded within, which also served as food for the larger animals. And the swarms of vermin, such as cockroaches, were beyond reckoning.

Add Alex Fender into the mix, and the fun begins.

Sometime in the 1970's, Alex decided to set the dump on fire – but the fire had consequences. All the creatures living in there had to have somewhere to go. The residential houses that backed up to the dump were the first to feel the tidal wave of shrieking, clawing, scurrying, foulness that poured into their homes, yards, and streets. Wave after wave of bugs and animals fled in mindless terror,

Despite the best efforts of the entire metroplex fire department, the fire could not be put out. They decided to let it burn itself out – which took a full year. The cause of the fire was attributed to "spontaneous combustion".

As time passed, the river deposited thousand of seeds into this mountain of manure and potash. Today, this area is renowned as the nation's largest hardwood forest. It is now a tourist attraction, sporting nature trails, equestrian rides and Audubon studies, which are just some of the many features available in what was the nation's largest illegal dump.

Axel attended a gala event some thirty-nine years after he set the dump on fire. The occasion was to mark the official opening of the area to the public. The event was attended by the richest and most powerful people in the city. Did I mention that Axel was not a guest? He was there serving drinks.

True to form, Axel spiked the punch with alcohol. In addition, he poured in a rather generous amount of "witch hazel". This substance is not supposed to be taken internally because it causes gas. Lots of gas.

Being a formal event, everyone was in tuxedoes and evening gowns. The alcohol in the drinks relaxed everyone so much; they just couldn't control the gas.

People would break into laughter about something and then fart like a bay mule. This only caused more hysterics and more farts. It appeared that Axel had created perpetual motion.

While preparing for this occasion, Axel had put on his old dress pants, only to discover white spots all over the legs. On closer examination, the white spots proved to be moth holes. The "white" was his skin showing through. He solved this situation with a black "Marks-a-Lot" to his skin, and no one was the wiser.

During the party, Axel got into a fight with a couple of obnoxious drunks. The sight of Axel fighting two people at once was very interesting. He would tell them where he was going to hit them – and he was so fast that neither drunk could prevent it. All in all, it was a successful, fun-filled night for Axel, with excitement for all, a time to be remembered.

Not to be denied, Casanova Goodbody crashed the party by slipping in through the servant's entrance. He had glued a small mirror to the toe of his shoe. During a conversation with a woman, he would slowly slide his foot next to hers in order to look up her dress. He was cured of this bad practice when one lady stomped his toes with her spiked heels.

By the event's conclusion, Casanova was roaring drunk and had to be dragged to the car in a completely inebriated condition. While people were loading him into the back seat, he shouted at a nearby group of people, "She's got a pussy!" He was told by the group to shut up. This only made him worse. In an attempt to distance himself, the driver of Casanova's car was peeling out, throwing gravel everywhere as Casonova hung his upper body out the back window shouting, "She's got a stinky, fishy pussy!"

They had pulled into a truck stop on the way home to get Casanova some coffee and attempt to sober him up. B.O. Sharp was watching after him by now and things had settled down some. It was about two AM. All the bars were closing and so all the drunks were out.

A very bored and tired waitress approached Casanova's group to take their order. Casanova slurred at her, "I loves ya!" The waitress didn't even flinch and replied, "I'm so proud!"

As Casanova began to sober up, B.O. confided a very confidential matter to him.

"Casanova," he said, "I fucked a woman once!"

"Once?" replied Casanova. "What the hell is once? Why, it's not even considered polite to fuck a woman just once!"

Casanova had recently gotten caught by his latest girlfriend. Suspecting something was going on, she broke into the house only to discover him in bed with her sister, which resulted in a horrible fight. Casanova retreated from the house and hid until things blew over.

A few days later both sisters, unable to settle the matter, decided to consult their mother about reconciliation. Upon arrival at their mother's house, they found Casanova in bed with her. The two girls just looked at one another and said, "You don't suppose he knows where Dad lives, do you?"

While still in high school, Animal-X decided he wanted to learn weight lifting. Since there was no facility for such activity in Briar Patch, Animal walked seven miles to the nearest place to work out. Eventually, he would run seven miles unless it was leg day. He gave up sleeping in his bed because he said it made him soft. To his parent's bewilderment, he began to sleep on the floor. Finally, in desperation for help, his parents took him to a psychiatrist. After his first and only session, Animal stated, "Why should I listen to that psychiatrist? He doesn't even work out!"

After Animal and Bunny got married, he took her to his local gym facility, but Bunny was more interested in showing herself off than in training. She used the stair-stepper a lot, going up and down on it many times so that people could see her titties bounce (Real ones bounce.)

Within this gym were some lice of the spot known as "gym bums". People of this nature shun manual labor because it detracts from their training. They rarely work at all. Mostly, you'll see them in broken-down cars, receiving food stamps and welfare. A few of them become "queer bait". They will live with some homosexual who wants to "sponsor" them. The more successful ones get new cars, extensive wardrobes, and are even supplied with women for their services.

A couple of these less successful ones went over to visit Bunny while Animal was out working. They came back to the gym showing everyone pictures of Bunny naked and shots of them having sex with her.

The gym owner, one of Animal's closest friends, called these two gentlemen into his office for a conference. Under no circumstances were they to show these pictures or discuss this subject on his premises.

Bunny would never tell Animal she loved him. According to her, such admissions made her weak and vulnerable. The truth was that Bunny was incapable of loving another person. Animal would wait until deep into the night when Bunny was asleep to tell her he loved her, otherwise it caused problems.

Someone influential saw Bunny at the gym and got some publicity for her. As a result, she got her picture on the cover of a national magazine. Although this was a "flash-in-the-pan" for Bunny's career, she saw it as her ticket to stardom and greatness. She persuaded Animal to sell all of his belongings, including his work tools, and move to Hollywood so that she could become a movie star. Bunny had no talent beyond her looks. The chance of her becoming a movie star was about the same as a one-legged cat trying to bury a turd on a frozen lake. She was however, a cunning stunt! (You'll figure it out!)

All she found in Hollywood were the casting couches, which promised much and delivered nothing.

She and Animal finally ran out of money. She convinced Animal to do pornography in order to finance their stay in Hollywood. Animal didn't like the idea – but Bunny was going to leave him if he didn't cooperate. His biggest fear was losing her, so he agreed to do it. He had flashes of ancestral memories of Eve telling Adam, "Eat some of this apple or I'm going to run off with that good-looking snake over there." Or perhaps Delilah telling Samson to have some more wine.

At the last minute, Animal backed out of the deal. He just couldn't lower himself that far. Upon arriving at the studio, he discovered Bunny in the arms of some director. The man was rubbing her ass like he thought a genie was going to pop out of it.

To make a long story short, Bunny ran off with a cocaine dealer and Animal went back to Briar Patch, where he and B.O. Sharp did some serious weight lifting and body building together. After a year of this therapy, both men entered the nationals in their sport. B.O. in powerlifting and Animal in bodybuilding. Both men placed fourth. Trophies were only given to the top three places. Upon returning to Briar Patch, they discovered someone had named a street after them. It was called "Fourth Street".

Animal had a long talk with Casanova (Bunny's brother), about the situation he was going through with her. According to Casanova, women like Bunny have lots of offers from many men – meaning that women with exceptional looks have choices.

'For example", stated Casanova, "you're a good looking man with a big dick and an average income. However, a woman will dump a big dick every time for a small-dicked, ugly man if money is a factor. The really interesting thing is that after she's got the ugly, rich man and she has had a kid or two by him to ensure financial security, she will then try to screw the good looking man with the big dick. That way, she has the best of both worlds. The only question is, will you allow it?"

"No," said Animal, "I won't. But I will never be complete without her!"

Chapter 27

When Billy Bob McKnob was without a car, he would ride freight trains to his destinations. Getting on and off moving trains is best done when they slow down for curves or hills. Freight trains do not always stop in towns or places of you choosing. Therefore, one must develop a proper skill for disembarking or exiting a fast moving train.

The best way to get off a fast train is to jump in the direction that the train is traveling. This lessens the speed of the object leaving the source. Jumping against the direction the train is traveling would increase the speed of exiting and likely cause injury.

A smart person will get a running start before jumping. Start in the far corner of a box car and run at an angle toward the door.

Billy Bob knew to take a good look out the door before starting his run. In the past he had jumped into cactus patches and once when drunk, he leaped out of a moving train while it crossed a bridge over a canyon.

On this particular occasion he looked out the door and didn't see any cactus or bridges. By the time he made his run and leap, the train was passing a telephone pole. Although McKnob missed seeing it before the jump, he didn't miss it after he launched himself into space. He was never quiet "right" after this experience and became even more erratic.

Billy Bob McKnob never got around to observing any rules on transportation of a motor vehicle. Instead of inspection and registration stickers, he would tape old mayonnaise jar labels inside the driver's window. This would "pass" at a distance. And if he was arrested, "so what!" He also permanently removed the driver's side door as well as the car hood. These were seen by him as unnecessary because he had to open them too much. In addition to this, he usually was drunk when propelling this unlikely contrivance about the countryside. Upon hearing about the group MAD. (Mothers Against Drunk Drivers), he responded by creating something called (Drunk Drivers Against Mothers). He labeled it DAM!

One evening he and Firewater Barstool were riding in his contraption, loosely referred to as a "car," on backcountry roads. They were traveling down a long hill and saw a huge pile of gravel piled in the middle of the road at the bottom. As the car began to speed up, Billy Bob applied the brakes, only to discover that there <u>were</u> no brakes.

He mentioned this fact to Firewater and casually stepped out of his side of the vehicle while traveling, in excess of, 50 mph. Barstool looked over at the spot where Billy Bob was supposed to be and discovered that he was missing. Firewater was dumbfounded by this situation, so he responded by turning up the bottle for one more good, long drink before hitting the gravel pile and shooting through the windshield.

Both of them got to share a hospital room and it was anyone's guess as to which one was the most damaged.

Firewater Barstool's alcoholism continued to erode the man to the point of at least four trips to the "rubber-room." Rubber-rooms are always done in light pastel colors, which are meant to be soothing.

Barstool would go on "benders" (long bouts of drinking which could last for weeks). During these benders he ate very little and only quit drinking when he was asleep, or passed out!

Near the end of these benders, he would develop the DT's (delirium tremors). The DT's got so severe that he could not get the bottle, or glass to his mouth without spilling or dropping it. Firewater solved this problem by taking his tie and knotting it around his wrist. He would pass the tie behind his neck, grasp the glass with the tied wrist and pull the other end of the tie down. Thus raising the glass to his mouth without mishap.

Eventually even this innovative method would fail. At that point he would pour the liquor into a bowl and lap it like a dog.

When he became too dysfunctional for even this to work, it was time for the rubber-room. Rubber-rooms usually have a small window located in the door. Barstool would watch for any passers-by, be it a hospital attendant or any ordinary visitor. He would see someone and start to screech, "Help me, help me, I'm loosing my mother fucking mind!"

He became so bad that he was eventually confined to a "straight-jacket" at night. Someone can escape from one of these by raising their arms overhead. It is not easy and is best preformed upside down. The great Houdini did it regularly, hanging upside down from a rope. This made the trick look harder than it actually was. Houdini could dislocate his shoulders, at will, which was also a big plus for this stunt.

No one knows exactly how Firewater accomplished his escape. However, once released he proceeded to write on the nice pastel walls. Unfortunately he chose to write with his own excrement. His message on the walls was, "Jesus saves." He realized it was bad to write with shit, but he rationalized that since he wrote something good, it was therefore okay.

The week before Christmas, Animal got an unusual phone call. Bunny had moved to the metroplex and gotten herself arrested. It seems that she had been stopped for a routine license check and the computer found some very old, unpaid traffic tickets. Her fines were extensive and absolutely no friend or family member was in any financial position to help her. Naturally she turned to Animal-X.

Animal knew if he didn't help her out she would loose her job and her apartment, since she was looking at extensive jail time. For a minute he was tempted to leave her there, but after all, it was Christmas.

Police departments will not accept checks so he drew $756.00 out of his savings account for this purpose. During the 1980's when this happened, $756.00 was a lot of money.

As soon as Bunny was released, he took her to a very fine restaurant and explained some facts to her. "I cannot continue to play this roll in you life. You are going to have to be all the way in my life, or all the way out of it," he said. "This is the last time you should depend on me if you are not going to be with me. I know you can't pay me back the money, and I don't expect it." Bunny's response was that she needed some time to think about it. She said she had a girl friend who owned a travel agency in L. A. and she was paying for Bunny's trip to see her. Bunny would think about what to do while she was in L. A. over the weekend.

When she returned from the trip, Animal phoned her, but she still didn't have an answer for him.

Bunny never realized how many people liked Animal, and how well thought of he was. She began to "run her mouth" in a health club about her trip to L. A. with a local businessman who paid for everything. It seems that she and her "man friend" left the metroplex the same day Animal got her out of jail. There never was a girlfriend who owned a travel agency! The gym community is small enough that someone told Animal about this indiscretion immediately.

He and Bunny had plans for Christmas, so he said nothing about the situation until after the holidays. He then asked her if she had anything she wanted to tell him. When she said "no," he calmly laid all her lies and cheating out in the sunlight. He then asked her why she didn't get this guy to get her out of jail since they were going to LA?

Her response was that the trip didn't cost the man anything because his business paid for it and besides, she wanted to see LA.

"You expect me to believe some man took you to LA for no reason," said Animal. "Oh, he tried, but I didn't give him any. I hardly ever see him," replied Bunny.

"How can I trust you," commented Animal, "you've already proven you'll lie to me. It's bad enough to do this, but you did it the same day I paid you out of jail. All I've ever done for you has just made you worse because I rewarded your behavior."

Bunny continued to attempt to get back into Animals life for years after, but he had finally had enough! Apparently he was the only person who had always been there for her. No one else would put up with her for any length of time. Bunny had finally destroyed the best thing she ever had. In the fullness of time, she ended up with illegitimate children, alone, and on welfare.

When Bookworm was in the first grade the school took the students on field trips to various places.

One day the boy came in from school and told his dad, "They took us on a field trip today." "Is that so," replied the father. "Where did you go?" "We went to a funeral home," responded Bookworm. "Well," thought his dad, "I guess it's good that their learning about some of the unpleasant facts of this life." Then Bookworm remarked, "I didn't like being made to hug those people!" "Damn," thought the dad, "their having those kids hug corpses, that's just too much!" The next day Bookworm's father called the school about the matter. He was thinking about going to the school to "Kick-some-ass" but figured he should call first, just in case he was wrong. Sure enough, the field trip had been to a nursing home, not a funeral home. Bookworm's dad explained to him that a nursing home is one step above a funeral home.

Casanova had persuaded a new woman to go on a picnic with him. After the meal he got the clothes off the wench and was doing their thing in the grass. The woman began to buck like a horse, scream, and gyrate in all directions. "Damn," thought Casanova, "I'm really doing this one some good." He soon found out the reason for her display was not his sexual prowess. It appeared that his choice of spots was badly chosen, as both of them were on top of a red ant mound.

Not to be easily discouraged, Casanova's next spot of choice was on top of the picnic table.

Now it just so happened that Bookworm's family was helping clean the park that day and were out picking up trash. The father was about one hundred yards ahead of the rest of the family when he came around the corner and saw two people madly screwing on top of the picnic table in plain sight. "My God," thought Bookworm's dad, "I can't let my family walk into something like this." Not knowing what else to do, he stuck the trash he was carrying into the dumpster and loudly slammed the lid. Then he retreated out of sight. By the time his family arrived, Casanova and the woman were both fully clothed and looking very innocent.

There was an elderly woman living in Briar Patch who had suffered a stroke. Half her face was paralyzed and she disliked going out in public. She began to have all her food delivered to her residence and eventually became a complete agoraphobic recluse.

Jimmy the Louse decided that he was going to get that old woman to come out of her house. It was something he became obsessed with. When none of his tricks of persuasion worked, he decided to set her house on fire and call the fire department.

Arriving at the residence, the firemen couldn't persuade the woman to leave the house any more than Louse could. They had to chop the door down and chase her through the place. Finally capturing the frantic creature, they had to fight her all the way out of the house. She bit, scratched, kicked and screamed. Eventually enough of them drug her outside, where upon she escaped and ran down the street yelling, "You're not sending me to a nuthouse!"

The fire was put out and she moved back in the house. However, quite a crowd had gathered during the "performance," and it was agreed by all attending that it was a great show.

There were other Creature clans scattered about the country. As the local clan was named after animals, there was another clan east of this one that was named for internal organs. There was Heart, Liver, Appendix, Spleen, Kidney, etc. There was even one named Bowels. Bowels tolerated the label, but felt that it was a "Shitty name."

Further east there was another clan named for external body parts. There was Ear, Toe, Navel, and a pair of twins named Right and Left Nut. The last Creature born to the clan must have been hard pressed for a name as they were running out of parts, so he was named Rectum. The name may have affected him negatively, as most people said he was an Ass-Hole!

If the Creatures ever took a meal in public, they had some very strict rules of conduct; never bite the hostess on the tit. Never wipe your ass on the curtains, and never scratch your nuts with the salad fork! The regular fork is all right, but not the salad fork.

Boscoe generally wore his clothes long past time to discard them. He appeared in public positively threadbare. One day he went to the county court house on business. The woman behind the counter took one look at him and said, "Sir, the indigent line is around the corner." Boscoe was worth millions at the time, but bought newer attire anyway!

Axel Fender stuck a bumper sticker on Boscoe's car that said, "If you love Jesus honk!" Everywhere Boscoe went people were honking their asses off at him. Soon Boscoe, who was short tempered anyway, began to cuss them and give them "the bird." This was a strange contradiction to someone sporting a Jesus sticker on the bumper.

Animal-X and B.O. discovered that pet shops in large cities have city ordinances against selling skunks and coons. They, therefore, were forced to "bootleg" their skunks. All in all, they probably financially broke even in the skunk business.

After getting out of skunks, both men continued to live at the residence. It was at this point that burglaries began to occur. Their house was burglarized sixteen times before they were able to stop it. Their insurance company dropped their policy, labeling their place a "remote dwelling". Burglar bars were pried off windows. Alarms were neutralized by removing the outside electric meter. Wall safes were pried open. Dogs were poisoned or shot. One day, however, the burglar's luck ran out. Both men came home together and there was the pimple-faced doper plying his trade.

Animal and B.O. would be the last two people you would ever want to aggravate. The very sight of them caused the burglar to surrender with no resistance. Animal-X frightened the burglar further by pretending to be crazy. He pretended that he and B.O. were the three bears and that they had just caught Goldilocks in their house. He would say, "And the baby bear said, someone's been sleeping in my bed too and the bastard's still here!"

This particular burglar must have been quite at home in their place, because he had even brought his girlfriend and her cat along to help him steal. Animal and B.O. locked the woman in the closet and went to work on "Goldilocks", as they had named the burglar. They took away all his clothes and tied him to a chair. All-the-while continuing to act crazy and increasing the burglar's fears.

B.O. got a long thin wire. They ran one end of the wire around Mr. Burglar's scrotum, quite snugly. Animal hooked the other end of the wire to his pick-up battery. Both men continued to laugh insanely during this procedure. B.O. began to crank on that starter and the burglar began to "sing". Animal-X recorded on paper all the confessions of "Goldilocks". They discovered where all their stolen property had gone. They also cleared dozens of burglaries performed on other victims. In addition, they received valuable information for the police involving drug trafficking. Only at this point did they call the police. This event was the only time Briar Patch ever made the national news. Everyone loved it!

Goldilocks tried to bring suit against Animal and B.O., while his girlfriend claimed that she was raped. The prosecuting attorney couldn't even get a jury to agree to serve. All charges against B.O. and Animal were dropped. Incidentally, they were never burglarized again.

Years later Animal-X got a job working at a luxurious country club in the metroplex. Because of his "Macho" appearance, Animal was in charge of the club's gym. This club was in the richest part of town. Only the wealthiest, well-to-do people joined this exclusive establishment. Men and women had separate workout areas. Both gyms were attached to a heated pool and whirlpool area. Animal was conducting a tour of men and women one day.

An elderly man in his ninety's had lost control of his bowels while in the whirlpool. Someone had sent for maintenance to get the pool cleaned out. As Animal's group of rich folks got to the pool area, Animal noticed that the whirlpool's condition was unchanged. In fact it was still running with feces flying all around it. He tried to hurry his group by this area but was unsuccessful. "What's that stuff in the whirlpool?" asked one of the potential members. Animal wasn't about to tell then that some old man had recently taken a crap in the thing. Thinking quickly he said, "That's the same minerals that the hot springs in Arkansas has. We import them here for your convenience." The group had already had their token workout and since they were dressed for the occasion, all of them jumped into the whirlpool. That wasn't the worst of it. They began to rub the "minerals" all over their arms, legs, and faces. Thank goodness the temperature of the water had killed all of the bacteria. Animal sure-as-hell wasn't going to tell them the truth now! He was thinking, "This is probably the only time I'll ever see rich people rubbing themselves in shit. I hope they don't ask for it on a regular basis or develop a liking for it."

Animal-X received his size from his mother's side of the family. His mother's feet were so large she had to buy men's shoes to wear. Women's shoes just didn't seem to fit her unusual proportions. By the time Animal was

215

thirteen years old, he was too big and strong for his parents to discipline and he began to "act out". He was cured of this bad behavior by his mother. When Animal was asleep at around three a.m., his mom would sneak into his bedroom and beat hell out of him with a broom handle. The broom was one of those large diameter industrial brooms that could really do some damage. Animal stated, "You wake up disoriented because you don't know where you are. You can't understand where all this pain is coming from and you think you're in hell!"

His mother got her size from her dad, who was a Russian immigrant. The man was huge and reported to be very "scary" looking. When the maternal grandfather was a young man there were some convicts who escaped from the state penitentiary nearby his home. Animal's grandfather began to carry a loaded shotgun all the time in case he saw the convicts. He was going out to his barn one day and as soon as he opened the barn door he saw movement in the dimly lit barn interior. Certain that he was being attacked by the convicts; he unloaded with both barrels of the shotgun. It seems that there was an old dusty mirror stored in the barn and the man had actually shot the image of himself. Word of this spread and the man was unmercifully heckled about being so ugly he had scared himself.

A similar incident of random shooting involved Crash. Apparently she couldn't shoot any better than she could drive. Being hopelessly uncoordinated, Crash actually shot other people's targets instead of her own at the police gun range. Her frustration with her inability to hit a target resulted in wild arm and hand movements. Slinging her arms and holding a loaded pistol caused instructors and students to duck, dodge, and fall down. Crash was totally oblivious to all this. Soon no one would practice at the gun range if she was there.

Briar Patch had a small jail made of railroad crossties that set along side the railroad tract. It was practically never used since there was no law in town. There was that rare occasion when a drunk tramp got off the train and the leading citizens took it upon themselves to incarcerate him until he sobered up. During the night Axel Fender hooked a log chain to the jailhouse. He hooked the other end of the chain to the last car on the incoming train. Naturally, when the train took off the next morning, so did the jail. The train began to move slowly and sluggishly at first and the jail was eased off its foundation and slid onto the railroad tracks. As the train increased its speed the jailhouse began to bounce and leap wildly into the air. Within a mile of the ever-increasing activity, the jail simply flew apart in all directions. The tramp, not knowing where he was, or what was happening, shot out of the wreckage. He was never seen again and may still be running.

Axel Fender was driving his car to a distant city for some unusual auto parts he needed. B.O. Sharp was on the trip with him. B.O. had never been more than fifty miles from Briar Patch in any direction (except one time when he flew to Jamaica). No one thought anything of this, people just accepted it. As they began to near the fifty mile point from home, B.O. began to fidget and sweat. Finally he announced, "Don't go past the next town!" "What!" said Axel? "If you go past the next town, I'll jump out of the car," replied B.O. "Are you crazy?" asked Axel. "I just know I can't go past the next town" was all B.O. would say.

Realizing that B.O. was serious, Axel asked him, "What do you think will happen beyond the next town? Do you think we'll fall off the edge of the world?" B.O. began to panic. "I can't explain it, it's very embarrassing." Axel let B.O. out at a gas station and picked him up on the way back home.

B.O. had "agoraphobia," but no one recognized what it was then.

The town sage, Ladoit Shagnasty, had a theory regarding such things. In Mr. Shagnasty's opinion, all these things, such as agoraphobia, bulimia, anorexia and so on, are products of our lifestyle. Shagnasty went on to say that primitive man has no such problems. Can you imagine an agoraphobic cave man? How would he catch meat if he were afraid to leave the cave? A bulimic cave woman would be equally as absurd. After all, people who spend the bulk of their day searching for food are not going to make a habit of throwing up.

Shagnasty further stated that mankind was created to be a nomadic hunter-gatherer society. Small groups of people traveling about and occasional meeting with other similar groups. One million years ago people's life expectancy was an average of nineteen years. This is why today people mature sexually long before they do mentally and emotionally. Men have always had to work together in order to catch meat. This is the reason that men can co-operate with each other. Women were originally possessions of men and always see each other as competitors. According to Shagnasty, mankind has been eating meat for over a million years and vegetarians are not going to make us into something we are not.

In short, he states that this modern society we exist in is purely artificial. If Davy Crockett or Daniel Boone were alive today, they might be in asylums.

The mental-emotional disorders we now experience are an outgrowth of trying to live a lifestyle for which we were never designed.

About the Author

The author holds multiple degrees in physical education, sociology, and biology. His experiences have been many and they are varied. He has worked in Federal Corrections, been a professional model, a probation officer, director of physical therapy, and done professional scouting. He holds numerous physique titles on state and regional levels, as well as placing high nationally. Businesses he has owned and operated are as follows: South Pacific Imports, Inc., The Men and Women's Mid-America Physique Championships, a School of BodyBuilding and Certification, and a meat smoking business. He has served as a physique judge for the A.A.U. and the N.P.C. at all levels of competition, as well as a board member for numerous zoo organizations. Currently he resides in Sherman, Texas where he owns and operates Treetop Exotics, a private animal enterprise that supplies zoos and other private breeders.